THE TOYBREAKER

A gripping serial killer crime thriller

ROY CHESTER

JOFFE BOOKS

Revised edition 2016 by Joffe Books, London.

First published 2008 by Robert Hale.

www.joffebooks.com

This book is a work of fiction. Names, characters, businesses, organizations, places and events are either the product of the author's imagination or are used fictitiously. Any resemblance to actual persons, living or dead, events or locales is entirely coincidental. The spelling is British English.

978-1-911021-81-0

To Henry.

PROLOGUE

"A bottle of pop and two packets of cheese and onion crisps, please?"

"What kind of pop?" The woman behind the counter smiled at the man.

He was in his mid-twenties, tall, with black curly hair and bright blue eyes. He looked at the little boy standing next to him. "What do you think, Jason?"

The boy looked about five years old. Unlike the man his hair was blond, but he had the same bright blue eyes. He was dressed in a white T-shirt and jeans.

"Lemonade," he replied. "A big bottle. And can we have Kit Kats as well?"

"Having a picnic then?" the woman asked as she placed the items together on the glass counter top.

"Yes, Mrs Seeton." The man nodded. "We thought we'd go into the park while the weather's nice."

"That's one pound thirty-five, please." She put everything into a plastic bag and handed it to him.

The man slipped a rucksack off his shoulders and put the bag inside. Then he fumbled in his pocket, spread a small pile of coins on the counter and began to count through them laboriously. A crowd of teenagers standing behind started to make fun of him, mimicking his actions and calling out words like 'divvy' and 'mental.'

But they stopped as soon as Mrs Seeton told them to shut up or leave the shop. Then she turned her attention to the man and helped him count the money. "Oh dear. Not quite enough here, I'm afraid."

"What if we just have one Kit Kat?" the man asked eagerly.

"Yes, that will do." It wouldn't, but it was only a few pennies short and she scooped up the coins and put them in the till. "Have a nice time in the park."

She turned to the teenagers as the man left with the boy. "Now, what do you lot want?"

When she'd served them, the woman who was next in the queue moved forward. "Making fun of him again, were they?"

Mrs Seeton sighed. "Only to be expected, I suppose, really."

"Yes." The woman nodded her agreement. "They can be cruel at that age. Still, like you say, it's to be expected. Not all there, is he?"

"No, there's something missing, right enough. Bit slow, as you might say. But he's so marvellous with that little lad of his. And the boy worships the ground his dad walks on. No doubt it'll be different when he grows up, more's the pity. But for now it's a treat just to see them together."

* * *

Outside the shop, the little boy held the man's hand and jumped up and down, trying to avoid stepping on the lines of the paving stones as they walked. The man laughed and measured his own strides as he helped the boy evade the crowds. It was Saturday afternoon and the pavement was busy with shoppers, the air filled with a cacophony of noise and traffic fumes.

But when they reached the end of the street and turned a corner they entered another world. A world of Victorian gentility, faded now but still reflected in the crescent of small red brick villas that curved in front of a wide pavement dotted with tall plane trees and ornate lamp standards. Across the street, facing the villas, the land fell away in a grassy slope towards an area of old dock buildings. Beyond them in the distance the silver gleam of the river shimmered in the haze.

The man and the boy crossed the street and moved onto the slope. For a while they followed a path but then struck off to the side and entered a thicket of small tangled shrubs growing against a high brick wall. In the centre, there was a grassy space and they sat down.

It was their place. A sanctuary where they were completely hidden, shut off from the rest of the world.

The man sat down on the grass, slipped the rucksack off his shoulders and opened a large pocket in the front. From inside he took out a faded cloth, which looked as if it might have been an old curtain, and spread it on the ground. The boy knelt down and took the bottle of lemonade, the crisps and the single Kit Kat out of the rucksack. He placed them on the cloth, then rummaged in the rucksack again and pulled out a red plastic box and four small teddy bears. He sat the bears around the edge of the cloth and opened the plastic box. Inside there was a tea set; six tiny cups and saucers, six plates and a teapot. He carefully set a cup and saucer by the side of each of the bears, and put a plate in front of them. Then he put out two more settings.

"Ready." He turned to the man and smiled.

"So put the food out."

"Do you want to help?"

The man smiled and shook his head, knowing the boy liked to do this part of the ritual on his own. It made him feel grown up.

The boy opened one of the crisp packets and divided the contents among the plates in front of the bears, before pouring lemonade into the cups. For the next few minutes he pretended that the bears were enjoying the food as he and the man sang the 'Teddy Bears' Picnic.'

After that they started on their own picnic. At first the boy divided the remaining packet of crisps between the two empty plates and they ate them, washed down by lemonade. Then they finished off those on the plates in front of the bears.

"Daddy, do you want half of the Kit Kat?" The boy's voice had an anxious note.

The man touched his stomach. "I don't think I could eat another thing. I'm too full up after those crisps. You have it all."

"Well, if you're sure." The boy tore the wrapper off the bar and began to eat the biscuit fingers.

When he'd finished he collected the plates and cups from the bears, chatting to the animals as he did so. Then he sat down next to the man, and snuggled up to him.

"I want to tell you something." He whispered in the man's ear.

"Oh, and what's that?"

"My daddy's my best friend. My bestest friend ever."

The man ruffled the boy's hair and held him close, a great flood of love running through him

So much love that he thought his mind might burst.

* * *

For a while the boy slept, cradled in the crook of the man's arm. When he woke, he wanted to play and the man opened the rucksack again. This time he took out a number of toys, carefully selected by the boy before they left the house, and put them on the grass.

There was a small dumper truck, a lorry and a crane all in die-cast metal, and a model dock and tramp steamer both beautifully made out of brightly painted wood. To the side of the clearing there was a pile of sand on the grass. They'd put it there earlier in the summer and the boy placed the dumper truck and lorry in front it, then arranged the dock and the ship on the opposite side of the clearing.

For the next half hour he was content to play, digging out successive loads of sand with the dumper, transferring them to the lorry and moving them to the dock. Once there, he used a crane to transfer the sand to the open hold of the ship which he sailed to an island in the middle of the clearing.

As the boy played the man sat watching him. Despite the heat and the bright sky, the man felt a sense of grim foreboding invade his mind. Like a shadow crossing the sun.

For months he'd lived with the fear. With the threat. But now it had changed. Ever since he'd seen . . .

He forced his mind away from the terror. But it kept coming back. The sight of that room. The terrible knowledge of the threat it held. The threat hanging over the boy. Over the person who was the centre of his life.

He felt the tears behind his eyes as he thought of the danger that lay in wait. The boy knew. Not the nature of the threat, but enough to awaken some primeval sense of apprehension in him. And as if reading the man's thoughts he looked up.

"Is it time to go yet, Daddy? We mustn't be late. But we've been good, haven't we? And God won't be angry with us, will he?"

"No, he won't be angry."

"So we won't have to go to the room?" He started to shake then and tears formed in his eyes.

"No." The man bent down and took him in his arms. "You won't have to go to that room again. Not ever. Daddy promises that."

As he held the boy his own tears ran unchecked down his face.

CHAPTER 1

She could smell it as soon as she walked through the door. The smell of failure. It hung heavy in the air, and it was etched in the faces of the officers at the row of computer terminals set on the long bench that occupied much of the space in the outer open-plan office.

Garton was under siege. A mood of despair that had been caught a few days earlier by a banner headline in the *Garton Evening News*:

> *EVIL IS WALKING THE STREETS OF THE CITY, AND IT MUST BE STOPPED.*

But it wasn't being stopped. And day by day the tension increased.

Two men were waiting in an office on a raised dais at the far side of the open-plan section. Most of the floor of the dais was filled with flip charts on easels, and glass screens covered in coloured writing. The wall space was taken up by whiteboards, holding a series of photographs of numbered crime scenes, and large screens displaying digital images. White-coated technicians were moving around, adjusting the images on the screens and updating the information on the white boards and the glass screens. All very high-tech, she thought.

Every inch of space was utilised, and the office seemed to have been tacked on as an incidental. Inside, a wooden laminate desk with a computer terminal on the surface filled the centre of the floor, and the wall space was taken up with filing cabinets and rows of steel shelving bulging with cardboard archive boxes. Four red plastic bucket chairs, the only splash of colour in the room, were arranged around a low table under a window which overlooked the main floor of the Operations Centre.

She knocked on the glass-fronted door and entered the office. One of the men came forward.

"Hannah Nightingale?"

"Yes."

"David Mallory." He held out his hand. The handshake was firm, but the smile that came with it didn't reach his eyes.

"Morning, Chief Superintendent."

"Morning. I'm the senior investigating officer for the Toybreaker special investigation team." He nodded towards the other man. "And this is Detective Chief Inspector Falcon."

Another handshake, but no smile this time. Just a cool appraisal from eyes like flint.

"We were told you're assigned to the investigation as an offender profiler." The anger in Mallory's voice was barely below the surface.

"And you don't approve of profilers?"

"Makes no difference. This is a direct order from on high. You are to be given everything. And just because I don't . . ."

"Guv," Falcon interrupted before the chief superintendent could finish the sentence. "Perhaps we should have some coffee before we start the briefing."

Mallory grunted and walked over to the widow.

"Miss Nightingale?" Falcon asked.

"Yes, I'd like coffee, thank you."

Falcon busied himself around a coffee machine on top of one of the filing cabinets, and she took the chance to study the two men. Physically, they could have not been more different.

Mallory was comfortably dressed in brown sports coat and cord trousers, with a check shirt and blue tie. He was tall, in his late forties, and had the broad shouldered athletic physique of a man who looked after his body. He had a mass of dark curly hair and a nose that looked as if it had been broken a few times. But it was his eyes that caught her attention. They were blue, like washed-out denim, and there was something hidden in them. Not cynicism, she decided. More a wariness towards the world. As if nothing could ever surprise him again.

Falcon was young, late twenties at the most, with a skin of polished ebony. And he was dressed like a fashion model in a dark grey beautifully cut pinstriped suit, grey shirt and silver grey tie. Private resources, Hannah guessed, unless they were paying policemen a lot more than she thought these days. His head was shaven and his features finely chiselled.

Falcon set three mugs of coffee on the table, together with a tray holding sachets of sugar, tiny cartons of cream and plastic spoons. The three of them sat down and Falcon passed one of the mugs to Hannah after she'd put her briefcase on the floor by her side.

"Cream, sugar?" Falcon indicated the tray.

She shook her head. "No thanks. Black will be fine." She sipped the coffee. It was strong, but surprisingly good.

When she looked up she saw that the two men were watching her. This was some kind of a test, and she realised that the moment was important.

OK, she thought. You want to play macho games, we'll play macho games.

She put her coffee cup down and looked at Mallory, forcing herself to remain silent. For a long moment the chief superintendent returned her stare. Then he nodded to himself.

"Miss Nightingale, we've been told to brief you on this investigation."

"Yes." She wasn't prepared to give him anything yet.

"So," Mallory seemed to acknowledge that they were both probing. "This investigation is being run by the Crime Management Task force and as I said, I'm the SIO."

"What system are you employing to manage the investigation?"

Mallory nodded again, accepting her insider knowledge. "We're using the force's modification of HOLMES."

"That's the Home Office Large Major Enquiry System, isn't it?" She knew very well what HOLMES was. She was just making a point.

"Yes. Now if we can move on." Either she'd passed the test, or he'd tired of playing games "How much do you know about the Toybreaker case?"

But she wasn't ready yet. She reached down and lifted the briefcase onto the table, opened it and took out a small tape recorder. "I hope you won't mind if I record this briefing." She smiled sweetly. "Just to make certain I don't miss anything when I write up my notes later."

Mallory didn't appear at all fazed. "I've no objection to what I say being recorded."

"Good." Hannah switched the machine on. "Go ahead, Chief Superintendent."

"The Toybreaker is every parent's nightmare. The worst of all evils. A serial kidnapper on the loose who snatches young children from their homes. And always in the night. A phantom that seems to come and go as it pleases."

"You identify the criminal as a serial kidnapper. How many children have been abducted so far?"

"It started about six months ago, July the sixteenth to be exact, and to date five children have gone missing."

"Is it just abduction?"

Mallory's expression hardened. "We've been using the term kidnapper because there's no evidence to indicate anything to the contrary. Yet."

"No bodies have been found?"

"No, but on the other hand there haven't been any ransom notes either. But more important, the children who've been abducted don't come from the kind of families who could pay a ransom in the first place. No, the reason for these crimes is not financial gain. I'm certain of it. And so is the media. Which is why the city is so on edge."

"And the abductions? They're always the same."

"They always follow a pattern, yes. All the children are between one and two years old from single-parent families living on their own. Just the mother and one child. No other children, and no partner."

Hannah nodded. "Social level?"

"Again, all the same. Living on benefit in council flats."

"And the mothers? OK, they've all got a young child, all live without a partner, and all are on benefit. Maybe there's a pattern there. But is there anything else that links them together?"

"Nothing else we've been able to pick up. Two were white, two of mixed race, and one Afro-Caribbean. And they all lived in different parts of the city."

"Religion?"

"No common factor there."

"So the women are linked by the type of *lifestyle* they lead, but nothing ties them together as *individuals*. Right?"

"Not as far as we can tell. There's not one solitary thread linking them together. And believe me, we've looked for connections. We've taken their lives apart until there's nothing, and I mean nothing, we don't know about these women.

"What about the way the children were abducted?"

"Again, they all follow the same pattern."

"Can you explain the pattern in detail, please?"

"Each of the children was taken from their bed sometime in the night without their mothers knowing. I say sometime in the night because none of the mothers can be specific."

"Where were the mothers sleeping?"

"In separate rooms. All of them."

"And the children were taken without any disturbance?"

"It would seem so, yes."

"Isn't that strange?"

"On the face of it, yes. You'd expect kids to make some kind of noise if they're woken in the night. But forensics found traces of chloroform on all of the pillows. Whoever did this made sure those kids stayed out of it. Same pattern each time. And then there were the calling cards, of course."

"This Toybreaker thing, you mean?"

"Yes, that was what caught the imagination of the public."

"These calling cards, they were the same each time?"

"Yes and no. A wooden toy, in the form of a brightly painted clown puppet was left behind each time. And it was always smashed into pieces. The only difference was that when we rebuilt the clowns, we found they increased in size with each crime."

"Interesting." Hannah gazed away for a moment, then turned back to Mallory. "Anything else about the clowns?"

"Yes, they were all superbly carved. The work of a genuine artist apparently, although we can't identify the woodcarver. We released photographs of the puppets to the papers, local and nationals, and they were shown on TV. Then we swept the net wider and asked all forces to check their areas for a craftsman that might have done the work. Took a long time, and in the end it yielded zilch."

"What about the paint that was used on the clowns?"

"Another blank. It was the kind of enamel paint used for plastic models and it can be bought in any hobby shop and a lot of newsagents as well. There are over fifty outlets in Garton alone."

"When I asked if the calling cards were the same each time, you said 'yes and no.' You mean something else was left behind? In addition to the clowns, I mean?"

"Yes, a lock of hair cut from the child's head."

Hannah sat upright in her chair. "A lock of hair." She repeated the words. "But this isn't common knowledge. Why was it kept from the media?"

"Because it gave us a quick way of filtering out any nutters who claimed to be the Toybreaker. But there was more to it than just leaving a lock of hair at the crime scene."

"How do you mean, more to it?"

"In the first two incidents there was no hair left behind at all. It didn't start until the third abduction when a lock of hair was left on the child's pillow beside the broken clown. In the fourth, the lock was found on the floor by the bedroom door. And in the fifth, the last incident to date, the lock was sent to the mother by post later."

"Look, you said earlier that the city was on edge. How bad is it?"

"There's serious tension out there. And it's building up day by day. If we're not careful something might just snap soon. Vigilante gangs braying for blood. Lynch mobs on the prowl looking for paedophiles. It won't take much to make it happen, believe me."

"It's that bad?"

"Worse. Because after all this time we don't have a single suspect."

"What about the paedophiles? Whether the mobs go after them or not, they must be prime suspects, surely?"

"For sure. They were the first people we considered. We've checked out every known and suspected paedophile in the entire country. Both on and off the Sex Offenders Register. And it got us exactly nowhere. We've also looked for similar abductions on the national databases, but there were no hits there, either. No, it won't take much to ratchet up the tension to breaking point."

Hannah nodded. "Yes, I can see that." She was beginning to appreciate how far the situation had drifted.

Mallory looked at his watch. "Look, it's half past twelve now. This afternoon we can start going over all the stuff we've got. Scene-of-the-crime reports and on-site videos, evidence files, interview tapes, photographs. Then DCI Falcon will take you through all the data we have on computer. But right now, I suggest we go for lunch. Somewhere away from this place. I need a break."

Hannah nodded. "I'd like that. Maybe we can talk off the record."

Mallory looked at the tape recorder. "You mean without that bloody thing listening in."

But at least he was smiling, Hannah noticed. The first sign he'd shown that he was human.

CHAPTER 2

The pub was at the end of a street of mean terraced houses somewhere at the back of the city centre.

They left the car in a derelict litter-strewn space at the rear and went inside. There were men drinking at round plastic-topped tables scattered around the long room, and there was a lull in the background hum of conversation when the newcomers came in. Two women were standing behind the bar, and the older one watched the scene wearily.

Mallory was leading, and as they passed one of the tables a youth stood up. He had a shaven head and was wearing a denim jacket cut away at the shoulders to reveal a mass of tattoos on his thick arms. He moved out and deliberately knocked into Mallory. The Chief Superintendent kept on walking but the youth grabbed his shoulder and spun him round. He started to mouth something, but one of the men sitting at the table thrust out a hand and jerked him back, muttering something into his ear. The youth glared at Mallory, but he didn't get up again.

"Morning, Mr Mallory." The older woman behind the bar smiled warmly at him. She was in her mid-forties, with lacquered blond hair and thick make-up. “Haven’t seen you for a long time, what can I get you?”

“A pint of bitter.” Mallory looked at Hannah and she said she’d have a glass of white wine, and then at Falcon, who settled for a half of bitter. “And a plate of your roast beef sandwiches, please,” Mallory said. “We’ll have them in the snug. Don’t want to disturb your regulars, do we?”

“Who was that, Annie?” the girl asked as Mallory led the way into the back room.

“Bit before your time, love. But that was David Mallory. Chief Inspector, as he was when he ran the streets round here, but he’s moved up the ladder since then.”

“What was he like?”

The woman thought for a moment. “He was a bloody hard man. A good thief-catcher, but not above a bit of the rough stuff at times. Still people said he was fair. And he was respected, I’ll say that for him.”

“So what’s he doing around here now then?”

The other woman laughed. “I don’t know, but it’s got some of them buggers worried.” She indicated the people at the tables. “You do the drinks and I’ll make the sandwiches. Fond of a good sandwich is Mr Mallory.”

The snug was a small room, dimly lit by a dirty window with a steel mesh on the outer side. They sat down at a dark wooden table and the young girl from the bar brought the drinks through.

Falcon took a sip of his drink and nodded appreciatively. “Good bitter.” Then he looked around the room. “But not exactly the Ritz, is it? So why bring us here?”

“My territory, CID used this pub a lot in the old days.”

Falcon looked surprised. “With all that low life drinking here?”

“Neutral ground, respected by both sides. They drank in the bar, we drank in here. It was a useful arrangement that could work to the advantage of both sides sometimes."

Falcon shook his head. "You're joking."

"No, I'm not." Mallory grinned. "But a set-up like that wouldn't be allowed nowadays, of course. Not under all the new codes of practice. But it was a different world then, and both sides knew where they stood."

"Excuse me, but this is definitely Dixon of Dock Green."

Hannah looked from one to the other. These were different people to the uptight officers who'd talked to her earlier. And she had a feeling that it was more than just relaxing over a drink. It was a kind of therapy. A therapy they both badly needed.

"Chief Superintendent, have you worked with a profiler before?" she said.

"No, can't say I've ever worked with a shrink." Mallory shook his head. "And the name's David, by the way."

"OK, David. But I take it you've got no faith in shrinks?"

He took a long pull at his pint. "I've been in court too many times when evil villains, and I do mean evil, have got away with 'unfit to plead on the grounds of diminished responsibility' because they've fooled well-meaning psychiatrists. And—"

He was interrupted by the landlady as she came in carrying a metal tray with a platter of sandwiches, a large bowl of chips and various condiments. She left the tray at the end of the table and asked if anyone wanted more drinks. Mallory and Falcon ordered the same again, but Hannah settled for a tonic.

For the next few minutes they concentrated on eating the food. As she reached over for another sandwich, Hannah smiled at Mallory. "These really are excellent. Perhaps the food was the reason you came here."

"I must admit it was good to know we could get a decent snack, the hours we used to work."

"What do you mean, used to?" Falcon growled.

Hannah picked up the undercurrent. "This investigation's getting to you, isn't it?"

He glanced quickly at Mallory. "You could say that. Yes, you definitely could say that."

"Look." Mallory twisted his glass round in his hand. "The investigation has put pressure on both of us. Massive pressure. That's par for the course. So what's different this time? I'll tell you what's different. We're no nearer to pinning down the Toybreaker that we were at the start of the investigation — six months ago. And take my word for it, that generates all kinds of pressure."

"I can understand that. But with all the facilities at your disposal you must have made some progress, surely?"

"'All the facilities at our disposal.'" Mallory considered the words. "Yes, we have all the facilities, no doubt about that. A first-class experienced team with every modern aid available to the police. We've got the best forensics, the best state-of-the-art data accessing and processing systems, the best expert IT advice. You want to go back to visit the crime scenes, we got videos of each one. You want data on a particular criminal sub-set, we got access to all the Home Office and National Criminal Intelligence Service databases. And the entire investigation is being carried out under a procedure designed to assess *Performance Management*, which means it's continually under review. Everything transparent and upfront. Like working in a bloody goldfish bowl. And we've used all these facilities. But to answer your question." He shook his head. "No, I wouldn't say we've made much progress. That a fair assessment, Gary?"

Falcon sighed. "I'd say very fair. Very fair, indeed. This Toybreaker's not given us shit, if you'll forgive the expression."

"He's right," Mallory agreed. "Apart from the smashed clowns and the locks of hair that were left there deliberately, the only two things of interest found at any of the scenes of crime were the traces of chloroform and a number of mystery fibres."

"What were these mystery fibres?"

"They were identified as cotton, but the type was unknown. According to the techies, they may have come off some kind of cloth, and there was a suggestion it that might have been used to wrap the children in. But that's as far as they could go."

"Were the fibres found at all the crime scenes?"

"No, just at the last four."

"And there was nothing else at any of the scenes?"

"No." Mallory shook his head. "No sightings, no prints, no other fibres, no bodily fluids. Nothing. Or at least, nothing we could make anything of."

"What about CCTV footage?"

"Again, nothing. Two of the blocks of flats had cameras installed to cover the main entrances because of past vandalism, but the Toybreaker must have got in and out some other way. And he wasn't picked up on any local CCTV cameras, either."

"Frustrating."

"True, although we did think we had a possible avenue of inquiry at one time."

"And what was that?" Hannah leaned forward across the table.

"The victims. They were all kids from one-parent families, but they lived at different locations. So who would have access to that kind of information?"

"Social workers, doctor's surgeries, health visitors."

"That's right. But like I said, there were no common factors among the victims. None of them had the same doctor, none of them were on the social services 'at risk' register, and none of them had been visited by the same health worker. So all the preliminary checks, the easy stuff, revealed nothing. Right, Gary?"

Falcon nodded. "So we started to build up a database then. All the social workers and health visitors employed in the city are on it. And we checked all of them. Personal backgrounds, professional details, alibis for the times of the crimes. Everything. But nothing showed up. Then we tried to identify the source of the chloroform, but that got nowhere either. The healthcare line of inquiry's still open, but it's been put on hold."

"You said you'd looked at the case from every possible angle, but surely there's one that hasn't been explored yet?"

Mallory grinned, and turned to Falcon. "What can she possibly mean?"

"Well, I'm not sure I understand how the minds of shrinks work. Too complex for me to unravel." Falcon kept his face perfectly straight. "But I think the lady might just be referring to this hotshot psychological offender profiling thing."

Hannah laughed. "All right, you two. I'll make an allowance for the fact that you're both obviously stressed out. But yes, I meant bringing in a profiler. But I take it you two don't agree with the idea?"

"Open mind," Mallory said. "Although underneath, I suppose I want police to do police work. Highly trained officers, like Gary here, but still members of the service."

"But maybe, just maybe, I can be of some help here."

"Lady," Mallory mimicked Falcon's voice. "Right now, if I thought it would lead to the arrest of the Toybreaker, I'd accept help from the fairies."

"Thank you." Sarcasm or not, Hannah recognised it as an acceptance of her position in the investigation. True, it was a grudging acceptance, but she guessed it was the best she was going to get. At least for the moment.

"So let's get back to the funhouse." Mallory began to stand up, but Hannah raised her hand.

"Just one more thing before we go, David. To clear the air. I understand the pressures when an investigation of this kind hits a brick wall. When the media are screaming for a result. But you two are experienced officers and, like you said, handling pressure is part of the job. So is it just lack of movement in the investigation, or is there something here you haven't told me about?"

"Shrewd." Mallory nodded to himself. Then he looked at Falcon.

The chief inspector shrugged. "Very shrewd. And maybe she should know."

"Right." Mallory sat down again. "I'm what you might call an old-fashioned copper. I used to run CID in the division round here. This was one of the toughest inner-city areas in the UK. Drugs, prostitution, protection rackets, armed robberies, gang warfare, violence on the streets. The lot. Tough villains, tough cops. The one called for the other. We knew them, they knew us. It's not in vogue now, of course. Not the acceptable face of the modern force."

"But they still promoted you," Hannah said.

"Oh yes. They made me deputy commander of the Crime Management Team. Because I'm a bloody good copper. But I still bucked against some of the new jargon-driven management strategies. Or rather, against the idiots on Executive Row who proposed them."

"Not a good career move, that." Falcon shook his head.

"True. Especially when I went too far and stuck my head over the parapet."

"Hold it there," Falcon interrupted. "Before you go any further, I would like to point out to the lady that it was to protect one of your officers. Since I'm sure modesty would prevent you making that point yourself."

"All right, so I felt a sense of loyalty to him." He turned back to Hannah. "It was a high level drugs investigation and we had a young DS working undercover in the ring that was running a large-scale supply racket. He'd taken a long time to work his way in and he was just starting to provide very high grade intelligence. Then I had information from a reliable informant that our man had been sussed and I wanted to pull him out. But I was overruled by the ACC running Crime Management. He wanted to keep the sergeant there for another twenty-four hours until we could set up an operation to move in on the ring. He was the boss, and we did what he said. Then a few hours later I received a message to go to a warehouse in the old dock area. Our man was there. He was strung up from a roof beam. Naked, with most of the flesh on his body burned away with what the pathologist thought was a blowtorch. A slow and very painful death."

"And you blamed the ACC for it?"

"I blamed him because it was his fault. There was an inquiry, but he told them that I had failed to inform him of the full extent of the risk to the DC. It was his word against mine, and in the end neither of us was disciplined. But he was responsible for the sergeant's death. And one night I got him on his own and decked him."

"You got disciplined for that, surely?" Hannah asked.

Mallory shook his head. "He didn't report it. If he had, I'd have been kicked off the force. But he knew that if he did make a complaint the whole can of worms would be opened up again and he didn't want to risk that. But as sure as God made little apples, there's someone up on Executive Row who hates my guts and wants to see my career in ashes."

"I see," Hannah said. "Like Gary said, not a good career move. But surely the ACC won't try to shunt the Toybreaker operation off the rails?"

Mallory smiled grimly. "Oh no, he's too much the consummate politician to do that. In fact, he's gone out of his way to make certain he's put together a good investigation. Me and young Gary here, we're the dream team."

"Dream team?"

"That's right. The old-fashioned in-your-face copper, and the modern IT specialist. For the record, Gary here is an expert on the use of computer techniques for criminal linkage identification. Although I have to confess, I don't really know what it all means."

Hannah looked at Falcon, expecting a sarcastic defend-your-territory reply. But there was obviously no rancour between the two officers, and Falcon just grinned.

"Anyway," Mallory went on. "The ACC's made sure people see that he's put the best team together. But in reality, he's just waiting for me to foul-up. And if that doesn't happen he'll settle for 'lack of sufficient progress' in the investigation. Any excuse to get me removed and have my reputation blackened. And in case you think I'm being paranoid, he's told me so himself."

"He admitted it?"

"Privately, yes. Because he knew the kind of extra pressure it would put me under. As if the case didn't generate enough pressure of its own anyway."

Well, well, Hannah thought, realising that she was being sucked into some kind of internal feud within the Garton force.

"So whatever happens, the bottom line is that you're not exactly flavour of the month with one of the top brass."

"Him and me both." Falcon grinned ironically.

"You too." Hannah felt the situation was beginning to take on a surreal quality.

"Yep, me too. Except that my problem doesn't stop on Executive Row. It runs right down to the cleaners in the canteen."

"But from what I heard you were . . ." Her voice trailed off as she sought the right words.

"The golden boy," Falcon finished the sentence for her. "A university law graduate on the fast track for promotion. And to put the icing on the cake, a black man.

The perfect recipe for a truly distinguished career in this modern politically correct police service. Except for one thing."

"And what's that?" She was getting tired of playing games.

"My name." He looked at her expectantly. "Falcon."

Falcon, of course. It clicked than. "Your father."

"That's right, lady. My daddy. You've heard of him, no doubt."

She'd heard of him. Conrad Falcon. The most prominent lawyer in the city, at least among the criminal fraternity. 'Villain's Friend' and 'Scourge of the Police' were among the names applied to him at various times by the media. And in addition to his law work, he was a nationally famous black activist and had served on the recent government commission on *Racial Equality in the Workplace.*

"You know he was personally responsible for the racial discrimination smear campaign that resulted in the resignation of the last chief constable."

"Yes, it was common knowledge at the time."

"Right, and for the smear campaign to succeed he needed a source hidden deep within the force."

"I can see that and . . ." she stopped.

"You got it. There was a widespread belief that I had been the mole supplying my daddy with sensitive information."

She understood then. The rest of the force would never forgive Falcon for that.

Never.

CHAPTER 3

Hannah needed to clear her head after sitting for hours in front of Falcon's computer screen in the enclosed atmosphere of the Operations Centre, and she decided to walk to her apartment. As she made her way through the streets towards the river she thought about the evening ahead. She was having dinner with Father David, and she made a mental note to write up her notes first so she could brief him on the Toybreaker case.

She smiled as she thought of Father David. In many ways he was her mentor, the teacher who had guided her and carefully refined her approach to criminal psychiatry. Father David was a Catholic priest with a small ministry in Stamford. He was also a highly qualified psychiatrist with a degree in medicine. The Church made use of his expertise in several ways, and he sometimes acted for his bishop as an exorcist. But he had made his reputation in the field of mental health. For years, with the full blessing of the Church, he'd run a small clinic for disturbed patients, attached to a hospital run by nuns. And Hannah had spent two years working with him at the clinic, after winning one of the greatly sought-after appointments there as a postgraduate research assistant. Only one appointment was made at a time, and Hannah had faced intense international competition to gain the place.

The two years at the clinic had been the hardest of her life. So much to learn, so much to understand, so much time needed for casework with the patients. Sometimes she didn't even know what day of the week it was. But she never regretted a single moment of the two years as Father David opened her mind in a way she'd never thought possible. In psychiatry his thinking was extremely modern, even edge-of-the-science in many respects. And he had pioneered several rehabilitation programmes that had gained him international prizes, and an acclaim that made him popular as a consultant and speaker. Despite all these worldly trappings of fame, he was above all else a priest with a life guided by faith, and that set him apart from some of his colleagues who believed he traded in the battle between good and evil.

The light was fading fast as Hannah walked through the tall glass doors at the entrance to the block of apartments. Inside, she called out a greeting to the uniformed security guard behind his desk in the foyer and took the lift to the top floor. The apartment was her pride and joy. It was in one of the dock warehouses that had recently been converted into housing units, and it had cost an arm and a leg. But whenever the thought troubled her, she justified the price on the grounds that it was a good investment.

The architects had kept to the original plan of the warehouse and the main living area was a long narrow room with cast-iron pillars supporting the low arched roof. One wall was covered with floor-to-ceiling shelves crammed with books, but almost the whole of the opposite wall was a large plate glass window with a stunning view of the sweep of the river into the estuary and out to sea. It was a view Hannah loved, and often she would just to sit and look out across the water as she wound down at the end of a working day. But now she was in a hurry to write up her notes and she drew the curtain across the window before taking a quick shower. When she'd dried herself she pulled on a towelling dressing gown and went into the kitchen to make tea. As soon as it was brewed she poured herself a cup and took it into the study, picking up her handbag on the way.

The study was small with a round window that overlooked a different stretch of the river, an aspect onto the open marshes on the far side of the water. The room was simply furnished, containing only a small curved-top desk, set under the window, with a swivel seat in front of it. A computer stood on the desk, with a small row of PC manuals on one side and a stack of discs and memory sticks on the other. Hannah put the cup of tea down on a brightly patterned tile, booted up the PC and plugged a fresh memory stick into a USB port.

She opened a file and named it *Toybreaker*. Then she took the recorder from her handbag and for the next hour she listened to the tape and transcribed her notes onto the file. When she'd read through them carefully she made a one page bullet-point summary of the data and printed it out.

In the bedroom she started to dress for the evening. Although she regarded Father David much more as a colleague and friend than a man of the Church, it was still difficult to know what to wear for a dinner date with a priest. In the end she selected a black suit, simple but elegant, and to break the severity she pinned on a red scarf. Then she looked at herself in the full-length mirror set into one of the doors in the wardrobe.

She was of medium height, slim but with a good figure she took care of by working out in the gym in the basement of the apartment block at least a couple of times each week. She moved her eyes up to the face framed in the shoulder-length dark hair. High cheekbones, a finely chiselled nose that was tilted at the tip, and a mouth that was really too large.

For a moment she grinned at the reflection. "Well," she muttered to herself, "You're not Kate Moss, but I suppose you'll do."

* * *

Father David was waiting in the bar at the restaurant, sitting at a table with a drink in front of him. He waved when he saw her and embraced her warmly when she came to the table.

He was 'out of uniform,' as he liked to put it, wearing a dark blue suit and black polo-neck sweater. But even without his ecclesiastical robes, he was an imposing figure. Tall and broad shouldered, with the features of his face strong under a mane of thick white hair. A powerful man who could have appeared intimidating. Except for his eyes. Kind understanding eyes that were full of compassion.

"Hannah," he held her at arm's length. "You're looking a little tired. Too much work and not enough play, I suspect."

She grimaced. "I have got rather a lot on at the moment, I must admit. What with the patients at the clinic, the course I'm running at the university, and the articles I'm trying to write, I never seem to have enough time. And now there's a new case I'd like to talk to you about. Something that only came up today."

"Whoa, slow down, young lady." He gestured with his hand and a waiter came over from behind the bar.

"A gin and tonic, I think." Father David looked at Hannah, who nodded with a smile. "And I'll have another of the same, please."

When the drinks came Father David lifted his glass. "Cheers, and here's to a lovely evening."

"Cheers." Hannah started to say something, but Father David raised his hand.

"When we agreed to meet this evening it was as old friends. To catch up on our lives. Not to talk shop. Now you tell me you want to discuss a new case. Well, I'm flattered you want my opinion and, of course, I'll be happy to help any way I can. But not now. After we've eaten we'll discuss professional matters. Until then, I insist we enjoy some of what I believe nowadays they call *prime time*."

Hannah grinned. "Actually, the expression's 'quality time,' but I agree, we'll leave work until later."

During the meal they brought each other up-to-date on what had been happening in their lives, and as usual Father David had her in fits of laughter with his wicked descriptions of a number of their colleagues. But then he became serious.

"You said when you first arrived that your workload was becoming oppressive. I understand that, and goodness knows I'm the last person to lecture anyone about becoming a workaholic. But with you it's different. You're an attractive young woman. So why don't I hear talk of men in your life? Is it because of Craig? Are you still trying to get over him?"

"I'll never get over him." She almost snapped the words at him.

He smiled gently, and took her hand. "Oh, but I think you will. However hard it is."

Craig. She still called his name in the darkness of the night when she couldn't sleep. When the memories came flooding back. Maybe Father David was right, she would get over him. But not just yet.

When they'd finished eating, they moved to the bar and the waiter brought coffee to them there.

Father David looked at Hannah. "So, tell me about this case you've taken on."

She took the sheet of paper from her handbag and quickly summarised the salient points of the Toybreaker investigation. Father David listened in silence, keeping his questions until he had the full picture.

When she'd finished he looked away for a moment. "Interesting." His voice was low pitched, almost as if he was talking to himself. "Of course, we have no evidence that this person has actually killed any of the abducted children."

"But you think it likely?"

"Oh, yes. I am absolutely certain of it. We can definitely assume we are dealing with a serial killer. And since most serial killers are men we'll assume the Toybreaker is as well. For the moment anyway."

"And the pattern of the crimes? They indicate the same person?"

"They would appear to do so, yes."

"What do you make of the signature that's left behind each time?"

"Ah, yes, the signature. The smashed wooden clown and the lock of hair are both interesting from a psychological point of view. So how do you interpret them?" He bounced the question back at her.

"The smashed clown is a sign of anger. The lock of hair, on the other hand, is a token of remembrance for the mother. A sign of perverted compassion almost."

Father David nodded. "Both strong symbolic messages. But there's a paradox in them. What we're seeing here are two faces of the Janus man. Different sides of the same personality. One side angry and violent, the other loving and caring."

"And they would produce a personality conflict?"

"They would be difficult to reconcile, certainly. But there's much more to it than that. I believe there is a genuine battle being fought in the deepest regions of this man's soul."

He saw Hannah was about to say something, but he held up his hand. "I know, we can argue about the concept of 'soul,' but the point here is that wherever it's taking place, this battle is tearing the Toybreaker apart. And the evidence for that is in the evolution of the successive crimes."

"The way the lock of hair was handled, you mean?"

"Exactly. For the first two incidents there was no lock of hair. Then in the third it was left on the child's pillow. In the fourth it was apparently thrown onto the floor, and in the fifth it was sent through the post later."

"So why wasn't a lock of hair left behind at the first two incidents?"

Father David smiled. "You expect all the answers now? As my friend Rabbi Cohen would say, 'like I'm an oracle?'"

She grinned. "No, of course not. But I'd still like your thoughts."

"All I can suggest at this stage is that something must have happened in the Toybreaker's life. Something traumatic enough to have initiated the battle between the caring and the angry sides in his personality. That's the most important factor in this whole scenario — the battle that's being fought out in the Toybreaker's mind. And based on the way things changed at the successive crime scenes, it appears the battle is heading up towards a climax."

"What will happen then?"

"I very much fear the anger side will become the victor."

"And the Toybreaker will commit further crimes?"

"Oh, yes. There's no doubt about that."

"So how can all this help in the police investigation?"

"In drawing up your offender profile, you mean?"

"Yes, that's why I've been called in."

"I think it can help a great deal. For one thing, I suggest you're looking for a person who has recently undergone a striking personality change. Perhaps because of a trauma associated with children. And that personality change will be evident to those who know him. Because as the Toybreaker switches from 'good' to 'evil' he will display a behaviour pattern which is characteristic of such a change."

"What kind of behaviour pattern?"

"As the conflict develops there will be progressively more and more anti-social tendencies. Withdrawal from the world around him into a pit of despair. But one thing is clear. The Toybreaker must be caught before the battle is finally brought to a conclusion. I cannot stress that too strongly."

"Why?" Hannah was shocked at the bleakness in his voice.

"Because once the battle is over he will be free. Free to do anything. Without any moral holdback whatsoever. And God help us because the Toybreaker will be completely out of control then."

CHAPTER 4

They sat at a table by a window overlooking the wild sweep of marshland that ran down towards the river, stretches of open water fringed by tall reeds that swayed in the wind. Under the pale, cloud-wracked sky there was a winter bleakness about the scene. A bleakness that was reflected in the expression of the man sitting across from Mallory in the balcony room of the riverside pub.

"David, for God's sake remember what I said. Don't underestimate Clayborn. It could be a fatal mistake."

"Is that why you asked me out here. To warn me about Clayborn again?"

"Partly, yes. I wasn't sure you took me seriously enough the first time. I know the inquiry into the death of the DC cleared Clayborn, but he has enough reason to hate you because it was you that forced the inquiry in the first place by blaming him for what happened. And it didn't help when he realised that people were queuing up to believe your version of events."

Mallory smiled, but there was no humour in it. "Oh, I took you seriously enough, and I wouldn't put anything past that bastard."

"I'm glad you understand. But bringing in the profiler has upped the stakes. You're getting drawn deeper and deeper into Clayborn's web now. And unless you're very careful you'll be too far in to escape."

"How does bringing Hannah Nightingale in draw me deeper into Clayborn's web?"

"It's a power game, David. That's how Executive Row works. Clayborn knows he can't get rid of you without just cause. But if there's still no progress in the investigation despite bringing in the profile, he can put a stronger case to the senior management team to have you pulled. And if that happens David Mallory's finished. Because the one thing they won't forgive is failure."

"Bloody politics." Mallory looked out of the window for a moment, watching the birds circling the marsh. "So it's just as well I've got you watching my back."

"I'll do what I can, you know that. I'm on the senior management team and I can keep you informed, warn you of threats. I'm happy to do that. And it's not just a question of favours being repaid either. We go back too far for that. So I *can* watch your back for you. But make no mistake. After a certain point, I won't be able to protect you any longer." He paused to let the words sink in. "And there's a good reason for that. Something they don't intend to tell you about. Not yet anyway."

Mallory felt the alarm bells ringing. "And what's that?"

"When they brought in Hannah Nightingale, Clayborn persuaded them to set a time limit on you. You and Falcon. You've got four weeks. Four weeks to demonstrate substantial progress has been made."

"And if we can't do that?" Mallory asked, although the answer was obvious enough.

"You'll both be replaced. And there'll be no doubt about where the responsibility for the failure of the investigation lies. It'll be a case of lambs to the slaughter. And believe me, they'll make a big media event out of it.

So they can point out the failure is yours, not theirs. That way they protect themselves. It's called survival."

Mallory was thinking about that when his cell phone rang. It was the Operations Centre.

The Toybreaker had made contact.

CHAPTER 5

Mallory and Falcon stood in the shadows on the street corner, looking across the small pedestrianised square. It was after midnight and the place was deserted now, but the empty stillness was an illusion. The square was completely sealed off, and the surrounding streets were alive with police vans and teams of officers on standby.

There was a sudden movement in the shadows and two uniformed officers appeared escorting Hannah Nightingale.

"What's happened?" she asked Mallory. "The call from the Operations Centre was vague."

"The Toybreaker's been in contact."

"How?"

"A message. It was addressed to the police officer in charge of the Toybreaker investigation, and we have a special arrangement with the post office to give priority to any mail of that kind. Which is why we got the letter so late at night."

"How do you know it's genuine?"

"He mentions the lock of hair left at the crime scenes. The one detail that was withheld from the media. There's no doubt the letter came from the Toybreaker."

"So what did it say?"

"That a sign had been left in the Cape of Good Hope Museum."

"What kind of a sign?"

"The letter's being checked out by forensics, but I made a copy for you." He took a sheet of paper from his pocket and passed it to her. The message was composed of letters cut out of what appeared to be a newspaper.

> Eyes have they, but they cannot see. The lock of hair was for love. But the eyes are for power. You will find the sign in the Cape of Good Hope Museum among the memories of children who were also taken from their parents.
> I will act again. Soon.

"Eyes have they, but they cannot see," Hannah repeated the words. "Biblical, I think." Then a thought struck her. "They must have CCTV inside the museum, so does this give us the chance of identifying whoever left the message there?"

Mallory grinned ruefully. "Oh, yes, they have CCTV. But no, it doesn't give us the chance of identifying anybody. Because as soon as the letter came in we liaised with the chief of the council security force and he told us that the system in the Cape of Good Hope Museum has been down for the last six months. Unlike the main museum, they don't have to protect priceless works of art, so with all the cutbacks, fixing the security cameras in there isn't a high priority."

"So what's happening?"

Mallory looked across the square. On the far side the façade was dominated by the outline of the Jamon Museum, an elegant Greek-style edifice erected with funds bequeathed to the city by an eighteenth century textile baron. But Mallory concentrated on a building to the right of the main museum. It was smaller but still retained the Greek theme, a temple with tall columns supporting the stone portico.

"The building's being checked out by the bomb squad protected by an armed response unit. And until they give us the all clear, we wait here."

"What made the Toybreaker pick on this museum?" Falcon asked.

"It's a memorial to the children who were killed when the SS *Cape of Good Hope* was torpedoed in the Atlantic early in the Second World War." It was Hannah who answered him. "The ship was taking them to a new life in Canada. Over two hundred children were lost when the ship went down, and the Toybreaker obviously sees the museum as some kind of symbolic location. A place which is sacred to the death of little children taken from their parents."

At that moment Mallory's radio buzzed. He acknowledged with his call sign and listened as the message came through. Then he turned to Falcon.

"That was the commander of the bomb squad. We're cleared to go in, but the teams are staying put until we complete our search."

The museum was on two floors. The ground floor was largely given over to background material and, in particular, to the minutiae of everyday life in a war-torn country. It was designed for educational visits, and had a hands-on interactive format so that children could experience what it was like to live in wartime. There were exhibits on the bombing of the major cities in the UK, the evacuation of the children away from danger, and their lives in the countryside. But a search of the exhibits revealed nothing out of the ordinary.

The main part of the upper floor was devoted to the tragedy of the sinking of the SS *Cape of Good Hope*. The central item was a large-scale model of the ship, with photographs showing the children in their accommodation areas, playing organised games in the sun on deck, watching films in the cinema, and working in the school rooms There was also an audio-visual display showing the sinking of the ship, which ran with sound and slide displays.

By the time they reached the final section, they'd still found no trace of anything left by the Toybreaker. The exhibits here told the individual stories of some of the children who'd sailed on the ship and as Hannah approached them she felt a rising tension, a physical stress that dragged at her legs.

There was something in the atmosphere. An overwhelming sense of young lives cut short. A feeling of loss that suddenly seemed very real in this shrine of sorrow. This must have been why the Toybreaker had chosen the place. If there was a message, then Hannah was sure now that it would have been left in this section. Where the powerful imagery worked its magic.

She began to walk around the exhibits, and eventually stopped in front of a display showing the life of a young girl from the slums of Garton. The girl's whole life was catalogued there. The harsh poverty of the environment was caught in stark black-and-white photographs, heightened by the contrast between the overcrowded pre-war streets teeming with a mass of humanity and the stark emptiness of the bombed-out urban landscapes. There was a reconstruction of the type of poorly furnished house that the girl would have lived in, with samples of the clothes she would have worn.

Hannah saw it then. And she gasped, the sound caught somewhere deep in her throat. It was a calling card. But there was no attempt at communication here. Nothing but a savage announcement of unspeakable evil.

"What the hell is it?" Falcon reached out but suddenly jerked his hand back.

It sat there by the side of a rag doll that was meant to be handled by visitors as part of the exhibit. A small fat bottle containing a thick viscous liquid stained with streaks of dark red drawn-out into winding shapes. And in the centre, unmoving in the bed of fluid, were two eyes. The eyes of a small child.

It was an image that would stay with Hannah for the rest of her life.

CHAPTER 6

"Here." Father David handed her the glass. "It's medicinal." He walked back to the bar.

She didn't argue and drank the brandy straight down. It burned her throat and made her cough. But when it had settled she felt better.

Father David came back to the table and this time he was carrying a small tray with two cups of coffee on it.

"Both black and strong. It's a good job this bar stays open until the small hours. Otherwise we would have had to meet in my room, and what would people have said then?"

She grinned at his feeble attempt at a joke, knowing full well that it was for her benefit.

"I'll tell you what they'd say. That you were lucky to have pulled such an attractive girl at your age."

"Have you no shame at all, woman?" He laughed loudly. "But seriously, it's good to see you back in the land of the living. You had me worried when you phoned."

"I had myself worried too. What was in that museum touched off a memory. A memory of that other time."

"Ah, yes. That other time." His voice was soft, almost a whisper. "So tell me about tonight."

He sat back listening as Hannah explained what had happened at the museum. But as soon as she mentioned the eyes in the jar, he jerked forward.

"Dear God, no." The words were almost inaudible this time.

"What is it?" Something in his voice made her shudder.

"When you first told me about this case, I said that in my opinion a battle is being fought in the mind of the Toybreaker. A battle between good and evil that arose because the Toybreaker was undergoing a personality change as the result of some trauma, possibly involving children."

"And you want to change that assessment now?"

He sighed. "Not in principle, no. But . . ."

"But?"

"The imagery we saw tonight has notched everything up a gear. Taking out the eyes of a child is an act of . . ." He hesitated. "An act of what one of my colleagues in the priesthood once called '*too pure an evil*.' And I genuinely feel we have entered a new dimension here. An area on the edge of human behaviour."

"The Explorer?" She had to force the words out.

"Yes, you were quite right to be reminded of the past. The other time, as you called it."

The Explorer. That was the file name they'd given to the patient. A name chosen because he'd crossed boundaries of evil rarely crossed before, and in doing so he had moved into the unknown. And the name still filled her with dread.

It was after her time in America, and Hannah had returned to Father David's clinic, this time on a short-term contract. A patient had been referred there for assessment after being arrested on suspicion of carrying out terrible acts of torture on little children. He had presented as a rather sad individual; immature, emotionally sterile and unable to relate to adults. But there was something in his behaviour, an occasional faint shadow of an inner power, that Hannah had picked up. After several sessions with him she was convinced that it wasn't something he was deliberately hiding. It was there, but he didn't know it existed. A part of his mind that the Explorer had blocked off.

Hannah asked Father David to sit in with her at the sessions, and gradually the two of them had begun to move into the innermost recesses of the Explorer's mind. And as they did so they revealed a world of such evil that it shocked even Father David. The acts that the Explorer carried out on little children in the dark caves of his imagination crossed lines that defied every taboo in every culture. And worse, they mirrored the Explorer's real life crimes. Not just those he was accused of, but others stretching back over years. And the depth of depravity shook Hannah and made her fear for her own sanity.

It had only been the gentle counselling of Father David that had brought her back. He'd started by making her face the fact that because her profession would, by its nature, open up unparalleled evil, there would be times when she would have to protect her own mind by erecting barriers between herself, the therapist, and the patient during their contact. He'd insisted that such barriers would not only allow her to carry out her work objectively, they might even be necessary for the maintenance of her own sanity.

But somewhere deep inside her mind Hannah retained the remains of her contact with the Explorer. She had been drawn into the darkness, and the experience had damaged her.

"You think this case has parallels to the Explorer?" she forced the question out.

"In the depth of evil they both show, yes. The Toybreaker belongs to what is, thank God, a very small number of human beings, and after this I would say there is nothing he is incapable of. Nothing under Heaven. But I no longer believe that someone who could do that to the eyes of a child has had their personality changed as the result of a single traumatic event. However devastating it was."

"So what are you saying?"

"He may very well have been in remission until the trauma happened, but the probability is that the Toybreaker has killed before. And you must make the police see that . . ."

"So the trauma event acted as a trigger that set him off killing again."

"Yes, and your role in the investigation will be even more important now that we know the depth of evil involved."

"Evil, yes," Hannah sounded puzzled. "But if the Toybreaker was already capable of committing acts of such evil *before* the trigger event, then why did he have to go through the personality conflict? In other words, why did he take account of the feelings of the mothers by leaving them a lock of hair?"

Father David shook his head. "That is the paradox I mentioned before, but I'm afraid I can't explain it. Even so, at least one thing is clear. The Toybreaker may very well already have been a killer who was, as it were, in remission, but the trigger event must have been an exceptionally destructive trauma. Something so terrible that the evil in him was switched back on. And if we could identity what that event was, we would hold the key to the mind of the Toybreaker."

Hannah felt the stab of fear then. She would help the police by constructing a profile of the Toybreaker. But because of what the Explorer had done to her, she hoped to God she would never have to probe the recesses of the Toybreaker's mind in a face to face confrontation. Because she wasn't ready for that yet.

With an effort of will she forced herself to push the thought aside and concentrate on what Father David had said. To make sure she understood.

"Just to be clear, you think the Toybreaker has a history going back before the events in Garton?"

"This is not the first time he has been active, I'm certain of that. And one more thing."

"Yes."

"The paradox. The reason why he showed concern for the mothers. Everything may revolve around that. Everything."

Father David was right. Everything did revolve around the paradox. But it was a long time before they knew why.

CHAPTER 7

Mallory wanted a briefing as soon as possible to discuss the latest development but Hannah already had a heavy day scheduled at the clinic, full of meetings and group sessions with patients that she couldn't cancel. In the end, they agreed to have an early morning meeting at half past seven in Mallory's office.

"So what do you make of last night's little episode?" Mallory asked. They were sitting around the low table drinking coffee.

"Whoa, hold it there." Hannah had expected the question, but she was determined not to be rushed into any hasty judgements. "I've only just come into this remember, and I need time before I can make any useful contribution to the investigation."

"Fair enough. I accept that," Mallory said, but he still sounded disappointed. "So at this stage let's just toss a few ideas around. Why do you think the Toybreaker decided to send us the message?"

"It was a statement, not a message. It's very important to understand that."

"A statement of what?" Falcon asked.

"Of defiance. The Toybreaker now feels totally outside the rules of society. That's what the statement meant. From now on, he'll be capable of anything."

"Jesus." Falcon ran his hand across his eyes. "After seeing that jar I can believe it."

"So can I," Mallory agreed. "But I still don't understand why the Toybreaker deliberately showed us the eyes?"

"I suspect it was a show of power. He's showing us that he's driven out any compassion he had. Will you go public on this?"

"No," Mallory snapped out the word. "The priority here is that we keep it from the families. God knows, they've been through enough already. How the hell do you think they'll feel if they get to hear the Toybreaker's been tearing the eyes out of their children?" It was the first time Mallory had let the stress show openly.

"Do you keep in touch with the mothers from the earlier cases?"

"Oh, yes. Very close touch. The force has a family liaison unit set up for that kind of thing, and they've assigned an officer to each family to be their own personal liaison until this is finished. Anything we have, they learn before the media come out with it."

"And what about the media? Surely they'll have suspected something was going on last night?"

"For sure they will, since we blocked off half the city," Mallory dragged his voice back under control. "But I've already spoken to the press office and we'll put out a statement saying that acting on information received we searched the area, but that in the end we didn't find anything. That will keep the lid on this for the time being, but what I don't understand is why the Toybreaker put out a warning that he's about to strike again? Is he playing games with us?"

"Absolutely not. This is no game, believe me." Hannah shook her head. "The reason that he's openly bragging about taking his next victim is part of his power trip. To show us that the rules don't mean anything to him anymore."

"Last question. How long before you can come up with a profile on the Toybreaker?"

"Look, I understand how urgent this is, but I have to go slowly. And any profile drawn up at this time will only be a preliminary assessment."

"But you're certain there's nothing you can tell us now that will help nail this bastard?"

"I don't know whether it will help to nail him, or not. But there is something you should know. Something that *could* be crucial. The Toybreaker probably has a history."

"What do you mean?" Mallory leaned forward across the table. "He has a history?"

"It's unlikely that these abductions are the first time he's gone over the edge."

"Maybe this just might give us something." Falcon actually sounded upbeat. "We've got the local and national databases on all serious crimes against children over the past ten years. We've interrogated them once, but I'll get the computer whiz kids to go through them again. See if they've missed any connections in there."

* * *

When Hannah arrived at the flat that evening it was late and the long hard day had taken its toll.

She took a hot shower then made a quick salad with avocado and goats' cheese. She poured a glass of crisp Chardonnay from a bottle taken straight from the fridge and ate the makeshift meal on her lap in front of the television, catching up with the news. When she'd finished, she poured another glass of wine, took it into the study, and sat down in front of the computer.

Drawing up a psychological profile was a complicated procedure, as much down to intuition and experience as science. Hannah was only too well aware of that as she booted up the computer and slipped the Toybreaker memory stick into a port. She opened a second file, but as she sat there the blank screen only mocked her. She sipped at the wine and tried a strategy she'd often relied on in the past; she simply let her mind wander, making no attempt to discipline her thoughts.

Slowly, those random thoughts began to coalesce, and she found she kept returning to the paradox identified by Father David. *If the Toybreaker had a history as a serial killer, then why had he shown some form of compassion to the mothers in the last four abductions?*

Like Father David had said, the key to understanding the Toybreaker probably lay in answering that question.

But her mind was still blocked, and in the end she gave in and went to bed. She slept, but it was a sleep beset with dreams. Then, somewhere far away, she heard a noise. A noise which grew in intensity until she could hardly stand it. She opened her eyes, looking around wildly.

Then she realised the phone was ringing. When she lifted the receiver she heard Mallory's voice, curt and sharp.

The Toybreaker had taken another child.

CHAPTER 8

They sent a car to pick her up and when it pulled onto the flagged area in front of the block of flats three other vehicles were already there, blue lights flashing in the dawn murk.

Hannah was taken inside the building where Mallory and Falcon were waiting in a stairwell leading onto a short corridor. Ahead of them, a forensic team was moving around. They were dressed in white boiler suits with pointed hoods, plastic over-wraps covering their shoes and latex gloves extending halfway up their arms Hannah thought they looked like creatures from another planet.

Mallory nodded a greeting. He was wearing latex gloves and overshoes himself, and was carrying a plastic supermarket bag.

"We've already interviewed the mother. And just like all the others, she can't tell us anything of any use. It seems she put the child, a two-year-old girl by the way, in her cot last night as usual. But when she looked in this morning the cot was empty."

"Where is she now?" Hannah asked.

"With the woman in the next door flat. You want to talk to her?"

Hannah shook her head. "You guys are the experts. I doubt I could get anything else out of her. Best to let her be."

"So let's move on." Mallory didn't argue. "I've been inside the flat already, but the techics wanted to secure the scene before opening it up. They've done that now, and they're happy for us to go in if we're all wearing gloves and overshoes. Which they kindly provided."

He opened the plastic bag and doled out gloves and overshoes. When Hannah and Falcon had put them on, they followed Mallory into the corridor, ducking under the blue and white scene-of-crime tape that screened off the area. They stopped at the entrance to the first flat. Two long thin panels of frosted glass ran down each side of the upper half of the front door, and a circular hole had been cut in the bottom of the right-hand one. Mallory pushed the door open and Hannah and Falcon followed him into a narrow hall. They moved forward and stopped in front of an open door.

"This is the child's bedroom." Mallory pointed inside, and he and Falcon waited as Hannah edged forward.

The light was on and she looked around. According to Deacon Gauter, the ex-FBI agent who'd taught her everything she knew about criminal profiling, this was an important moment. The chance to see for herself the way the crime scene was arranged. To pick up any signals left behind, then to try and figure out if they could help her get inside the mind of the criminal.

She stayed quite still, her eyes tracking the room. The walls were yellow with pictures of animals stencilled on them, and the carpet was blue. A unit with books and stuffed toys on the shelves was against one wall and the child's cot was against the opposite wall. An elephant mobile hung from the ceiling above it. The normal room of a well-cared for child. Except that Hannah sensed something outside the normal framework.

She turned to Mallory. "Is it all right to go inside?"

"No problem, forensics have left the scene undisturbed so you could examine it. But they'll want to label and bag everything as evidence later, so they'd appreciate it if nothing was touched."

Hannah moved inside and stood by the side of the cot. Then she looked through the bars and saw the 'thing' on the pillow. The broken pieces of the wooden clown. She focussed on the head with its pointed hat, red cheeks and wide grinning mouth.

She moved round the rest of the room, drawing in the atmosphere. And in the end she realised what it was that was wrong.

Everything was too neat.

* * *

The café was across the street from the flat. It was small and run-down like the rest of the area, and several of the shops around it were boarded up

They were sitting at a table in the window, with mugs of steaming tea in front of them.

Mallory looked across at Hannah. "Did you pick anything up at the scene?"

"One or two things, yes. And I'll plug them in when I draw up a profile. But there's two points I should mention now. The first is that if the Toybreaker is anger-driven, then he controlled it well at the crime scene. The only evidence of anger was the broken clown on the pillow."

"And the second point?" Mallory asked.

For a moment Hannah didn't answer. Then she sighed. "That's what I didn't understand. Everything seemed so . . ." She searched for the right word. "So neat. It wasn't just that the Toybreaker hadn't disturbed anything. If you take a child out of a cot, you'd expect something to be out of place. But even the blankets had been neatly folded again."

"And what does that tell you?" Mallory said.

Hannah shook her head. "I don't know yet. But one thing's for sure. It's not the characteristic behaviour of an anger-driven psychopath."

"Maybe I can help there." Mallory smiled for the first time that morning. "I saved the best till last, as the words of the song go. I wanted you to see the crime scene without any preconceptions, and from what you just said I think I was right to hold back."

"Hold what back?"

"This time there was a sighting."

"A sighting?" Hannah leaned forward. "You mean someone actually saw who took the kid?"

"That's right. The witness is an old man. A Mr Goodall, who lives in a second floor flat. Apparently, he doesn't sleep well and he often gets up in the night. He likes a pipe, but it seems his wife suffers from asthma and he doesn't smoke in the flat. So last night, despite the cold, he went out on the balcony to light up. It was about half past three and he said after he'd been there about five minutes he heard a noise on the pavement and when he looked over the balcony he saw a figure come out of a ground floor flat carrying something wrapped in a blanket."

"Did he get a good look at this figure?" Hannah asked.

"He only saw them for a second. When they passed under a street light."

"And?" Hannah could hardly control her impatience.

"It shatters the preconception we had. The one that says most serial killers are men. That's why I kept quiet until you'd seen the inside of the flat."

"It was a woman?"

"Yes. A young woman, in her twenties, the witness thought. Around five foot six in height."

"A woman." Hannah looked away, her voice soft. "That might explain why everything in the baby's room was so neat." She turned back to Mallory. "Was there anything else about her?"

"Oh, yes, there was something else. She was wearing a nurse's uniform."

"A nurse's uniform?" Hannah was aware she was beginning to sound like an echo. "Another medical connection. And a woman trained to be neat. It makes sense."

"But that's only the half of it," Mallory said. "According to Mr Goodall it was an old-fashioned uniform with a red cross on the head dress. Just like those worn by the nurses in the First World War, he said. He knows that because apparently he's a bit of a military history buff."

"Did Mr Goodall call it in?" Hannah asked.

Mallory shrugged. "No, he didn't. Think about it. Would you tell the police you'd seen a woman dressed as a World War One nurse coming out of a block of flats at half past three in the morning? They'd think he'd been on the magic mushrooms No, he went back to bed, and he only told the uniform that was doing house-to-house when he called. But the nurse's outfit might account for the mystery cotton fibres found at the other scenes."

"Oh, and one other thing," Falcon added. "The woman was wearing a face mask. The kind of surgical mask they used to wear for operations."

CHAPTER 9

Hannah sat in front of the computer, trying to focus her thoughts.

Who was the Toybreaker? What kind of a person were they looking for? She let the questions wander in the spaces of her thoughts.

Slowly a pattern began to form as she sifted through the data. A pattern that she hoped would eventually allow her to enter the mind of the Toybreaker. To assume the personality of the 'nurse,' and think as she would think. Or, as Deacon Gauter had put it, 'to look into the eye of the storm.' Which in some strange way meant she had to empathise with a deviant. But after the experience with the Explorer she found the idea frightening, because it meant that once more she might have to touch the darkness on the extreme edge of human behaviour.

In the end, she was able to push the fear aside and focus her mind enough to start to draw up a preliminary assessment of the Toybreaker. But she would stress to Mallory that she didn't have enough data yet to put together a personality make-up.

When she'd put as much into the assessment as she could, she tidied it up into a series of bullet points.

THE TOYBREAKER:

Facts.

- The Toybreaker is female. Age mid-twenties to mid-thirties, height around five foot six.

- She's been seen in an old-fashioned nurse's uniform, so may have some connection to the medical profession.

- She targets single mothers, so must have access to data on their whereabouts.

- The wording of the note sent to the police suggests that she may have a religious background.

- She is organised enough to carry a kit with her to the crime scenes — e.g. glass cutters, scissors to snip the hair samples (when taken at the scene). Important because it could be argued that being this organised indicates that she is in control, and although she could well be suffering from a mental illness she could be considered by a court to be *legally* responsible for her actions.

- She carefully arranges each crime scene by leaving behind a broken toy clown and (sometimes) a lock of hair, but leaves everything neat and tidy — compulsive /obsessive syndrome?

Speculation.

- She has probably suffered a trauma that acted as a trigger, forcing her to become the Toybreaker.

- But the trigger is unlikely to have been responsible for such a high degree of 'evil' behaviour. So it is probable that she has a history of crimes against children, and that her evil side was simply re-activated by the trigger event.

- She is undergoing a personality change. The change is not complete yet, and it results in a conflict between compassion and anger. But there is strong evidence (e.g. the difference in the way the lock of hair is presented to the parent) that the anger side is prevailing.

- The victory of the angry side of her personality will give rise to a behaviour pattern in which she becomes more and more withdrawn from the world and falls into a pit of despair.

- She will have little insight into her condition, and it is probable that she will present as a nervous introvert.

- Her behaviour pattern is extremely dangerous because once the anger has taken over completely she will throw off all constraints and act outside the rules of normal society.

Comparison with known personality types.

- Could be important, but need to refer to relevant databases — action later.

Hannah was aware that the assessment contained certain words and concepts — like 'evil' and 'trigger event' — that needed to be defined in a much more rigorous way before they could be used professionally. But it was done deliberately, to avoid bewildering Mallory and Falcon with too much jargon.

She read through the assessment again, then added a list of questions at the end.

QUESTIONS REGARDING THE UNSUB:

1. Why does she choose to abduct children of that age?

2. Where does she get the information on the families from?

3. Why do the children simply disappear with no further word?

4. Why does she dress in the nurse's uniform and face mask? — *may be very important.*

5. What is the symbolic significance of the wooden clowns?

6. If she has a past history of crimes against children, why is she going through a personality conflict now? — *part of a paradox, and may be the most important unknown in the equation.*

As she read through the list she smiled, realising that she had unconsciously used the term UNSUB, FBI-speak for 'unknown subject,' that she'd picked up during her time at Deacon Gauter's clinic in the States.

It was a preliminary scan that was nowhere near complete, but it might give Mallory and Falcon something to work on. So she printed off two copies, including the set of questions, and put them in her briefcase to take to the meeting Mallory had called for the following morning.

But she was aware she was the new girl on the block, and that David Mallory was still sceptical about profiling.

CHAPTER 10

"SCUM, SCUM, SCUM, SCUM, SCUM, SCUM."

The words echoed along the narrow canyon of the street, screamed out to the cadence of the beating of sticks on dustbin lids. And the line of chanting figures moved slowly forward towards the police vans drawn up ahead.

It had been a close thing. The warning of trouble had given the police just enough time to bring in a riot squad and deploy them to block the street so the house could be isolated. The house where the known paedophile, the youth on the Sex Offenders Register, lived with his mother.

Now the police faced the crowd. A menacing phalanx in full riot gear, protected behind shields and with batons drawn. Behind, the street was closed off by a row of blue vans, their windscreens hidden behind steel mesh screens. In front, a lone officer holding a loudhailer faced the oncoming crowd. He started to issue a warning, but the words were drowned out by the chanting.

"SCUM, SCUM, SCUM, SCUM, SCUM, SCUM."

And still the crowd moved forward.

Then the first petrol bomb arced over the front rank of the demonstrators and burst into flame as it hit the cobbles just ahead of the police line. For a moment there was a stunned silence as the chanting died away and the progress of the line faltered. But the pressure from behind was too great and the front ranks stumbled forward. Several people went down, screaming as they were crushed under the feet of those thrown forward.

And the crowd became a mob.

The hard core of agitators had been careful to stay in the rear, but now they unleashed a fusillade of petrol bombs and moved against the police in a coordinated attack. In the narrow confines of the street the fighting was fierce and brutal, but the police were able to hold the line. Until a small group of agitators broke through and climbed over one of the vans.

They reached the house where the youth lived and were faced by more riot police drawn up across the small front lawn. The word went around that the youth and his mother had already been taken away. When the agitators heard it they vented their fury on the officers guarding the house.

The scenes of carnage went out onto the nation's television screens later that night. Through the drifting smoke images of inert bodies lying in the cobbled streets, wrecked vehicles, and bloodstained police officers were caught on camera. All illuminated in the flames from the burning house.

A crisis point had been reached, and the city was on the brink.

CHAPTER 11

Falcon parked the car in the space in front of the building and went inside. It was a new police station, built by the side of the magistrates' court in the small market town. There was no one on the desk but when he rang the bell a door at the end of corridor opened and a smart looking young WPC came out.

"Yes, sir, can I help?"

"Chief Inspector Falcon, Garton CID." He showed her his warrant card. "I'd like to speak to Sergeant Mike O'Brian. I know he's on duty because I checked."

"Is the sarge expecting you, sir?"

Falcon shook his head. "No, it's a surprise. A ghost from the past."

"The past? Yes, I'd heard he came here from the Garton force. He was in CID there, wasn't he?"

"He was indeed."

For a moment, Falcon thought she was going pry into O'Brian's past. It wasn't surprising really because he'd heard that the sergeant had built quite a reputation as a hard man out here in the woods. But in the end the WPC evidently thought better of it.

"Would you like to come through, sir."

Falcon shook his head. "No thanks. Just phone Sergeant O'Brian and tell him that someone at the desk wants to see him. Someone who wants to make an official complaint. But don't give him my name."

The WPC stiffened, then lifted one of the phones on the desk, dialled a number and repeated the message slowly to someone at the other end.

She listened for a moment. "No, Sarge, he refuses to give his name."

She put the phone down and turned to Falcon. "Can I inquire what the nature of the complaint, sir?"

Falcon shook his head. "It's personal."

She knew she shouldn't have asked, but it had been worth a try. The gossip about a complaint against the Iron Man would be round the station like wildfire anyway.

At that moment the door opened again and a man in a sergeant's uniform came through. He was a giant and seemed to fill the space behind the desk with his imposing presence. He ignored the WPC, opened a latch on the desk and moved to the other side where Falcon was waiting. For a long moment the two men just stood there staring at each other and the WPC began to think seriously about pressing the panic button and bringing up reinforcements before a fight broke out.

"What bloody complaint?" The sergeant growled out the words in a deep intimidating voice.

"A very serious one, I'm afraid, Sergeant. Last time you buggered off without paying your round."

O'Brian came forward, moving very fast for such a big man, and the WPC's finger touched the panic button. Then she stopped, gazing in wonder as her sergeant, the man with a reputation feared throughout the county, suddenly lifted the chief inspector off his feet in a great bear hug.

Falcon grinned at the WPC. "Meet the bastard who taught me everything I know about being a copper. And a lot more besides."

* * *

"Cheers." Falcon lifted his pint.

They were sitting by the side of a roaring fire in a pub on the outskirts of the market town. The place had undergone a recent makeover, all sham wooden beams and bookcases, with chintz-covered easy chairs scattered around the floor. 'You'll feel as if you're drinking in the living room of somebody's house.' O'Brian joked as Falcon drove them there. 'But the landlord keeps the best Guinness this side of the water, so he does.'

As they sat there he looked at Falcon and returned his greeting. "Cheers. And chief inspector now, is it? Never any holding back for you, was there?"

"You knew I was ambitious, Mike."

"That I did. You being a hotshot fast-track boy and all."

Falcon grinned "Never forgave me for that, did you?"

"You can't learn to become a bobby by getting a bloody university degree."

"Was that why you picked on me so much when I first joined CID? I never did ask?"

"No, I'll give you that, you didn't. You took it all, and then came back for more. But no, if you want the truth it wasn't because you were on the fast track. And before you ask, no, it wasn't because of your colour either."

"That was one thing I never doubted. So what was it then? Why did you pick on me like that?"

O'Brian shook his head. "You really don't know, do you?"

"No, I don't. And you never told me either."

"I didn't, did I. Let me get another drink." He stood up and walked over to the bar. When he came back he was carrying two more pints of Guinness.

"I'll order us a couple of steak sandwiches later. They're good here and they'll help mop up the drink. Don't want you getting picked up by the county traffic boys, do we? They'd love that. Make their day running in a

Garton DCI for driving under the influence." He took a long appreciative drink of his Guinness. "So what brings you out to the sticks."

"Got a problem, Mike. Wanted your advice."

"I'm listening."

Falcon smiled to himself. There was no suggestion of surprise from O'Brian that his advice should be sought by a senior officer. They'd been too close for that.

"You know about the Toybreaker case?"

"We may be out in the wilderness here, but we're not entirely cut off from the world. Yes, I've heard about the Toybreaker. And I know David Mallory's SIO on the case, with you as his deputy. Is it the investigation you want to talk about then?"

"Not exactly. It's all the baggage surrounding it. You heard about what happened to Steve Morton?"

"The last chief constable? Yes, he had to resign because he made a racist remark. So what was the feeling about that in the force?"

"There was a lot of resentment about the way he was treated. For one thing, the chief constable was a popular officer. He looked after the men under him, and he brought down crime in the city. And for another, he made that remark at a private social event, not in public. The only people present were members of the force. The feeling is, it should have stayed private."

"I don't accept that. He made the remark, he has to take the consequences. But how do you fit into this?"

"You know who led the campaign to get rid of the chief constable. The man who was fed the information on what happened at that social gathering?"

"Your old man. Conrad Falcon, no less. The friend of the poor downtrodden lawbreaker."

"That's right." Falcon was quiet for a moment. "Mike, I told you once why I wanted to be in the service. You remember what I said?"

"You said you wanted to make a difference. For the black minority. That was why you didn't go into the law. Because you felt you had more chance of making a difference in the police."

"And I thought I was beginning to make that difference. A black officer who was going up the chain of command not because he was black, but because he was good. But it's not easy, Mike."

"Nobody said it was going to be. But what's the problem now?"

"People think I'm the mole that exposed the chief constable. That it was me who told my father what went on at that private social event."

"You were there?"

"Yes, I was there."

"And were you the mole?"

"No, Mike, I wasn't."

"OK, I believe you. But I can see you're in a trap."

"For sure, I am. If I deny it, people would say I was lying to protect myself. Same goes for my father. If he said it wasn't me, nobody would believe him either. They'd say he was trying to protect his own son. No, the only way people *would* believe him, was if he actually revealed the name of the real source. And he won't do that."

O'Brian looked across at Falcon, and when he spoke his voice was surprisingly gentle. "Whether people think you're the mole isn't the problem, is it? Or, at least, it isn't the main problem."

Falcon shook his head. "I knew you'd see it. That's why I came here to talk. But you're right, the thing that's cutting me up isn't that people think I was the mole. It's because I know I wasn't."

"Jesus, Mary and Joseph, and they say the Irish talk in conundrums But this time, I do know what you mean. The chief constable made a racist remark. Public meeting or private gathering, it was made in front of other people. Maybe someone in that kind of high-profile job has no right to stay in office after making a remark like that. Because there must be some degree of prejudice behind it. So the mole exposed a real injustice, and you're wearing a hair shirt because as a high-ranking black officer you didn't openly expose the chief constable yourself. Is that it? You think you've betrayed the cause?"

"That's exactly what my father said. That I'd betrayed the cause."

"And you believe that."

"No. Or at least, I didn't at the time. OK, so the chief constable made a racist remark, although it was just a bad joke really. But I've heard enough of them during my career, and I always made a point of not being seen as continually moaning. Of not always being on the lookout for insults so that I could bring in the 'race police' every time I imagined someone was getting at me because of my colour. It's a very fine line, Mike, I know that. But this time I would have let things lie. Because I'm a realist. Black people should have the same kind of respect as anyone else, of course we should. And in an ideal world we would. But this world's far from ideal, and the reality is that the situation's only going to improve when people from the ethnic minorities prove we can do the top jobs. I wanted to be promoted because I was good, not because I was black."

"So you felt you would have ruined your career if you'd have been the whistle blower who brought the chief constable down. And you *would* have sabotaged your prospects, no doubt about that. But the decision you made was right."

"You think so?"

"I know so. You've worked bloody hard to get where you are, and you're a damned good copper. Look, you asked me earlier why I put you through the mill when you first joined CID. It was because I could see your potential. But that's all it was. *Potential.* I had to know there was steel underneath. And you had to prove it to yourself. And you did. You can get to the top on merit, and for what it's worth I believe you'll do a damn fine job. You could be a national icon. The first black chief constable. And that's what's important. The end-point. You would have been wrong to risk that for a short-term public relations exercise. So stop tearing yourself apart. To put it crudely, your best chance of helping the cause is to get up the ladder as high as you can."

"Thanks, Mike, that kind of support means a hell of a lot to me. But there's another problem here."

"And that is?"

"Like I said before, keeping quiet about the racist remark backfired. Because most people still think I was the mole. But the strange thing is, somebody up there in the corridors of power seems to be working on my side."

"What makes you think that?" O'Brian sounded surprised.

"Two reasons. First, I was discreetly warned off when I tried to make my own inquiries about the identity of the mole."

"Who warned you off?"

"I don't know."

O'Brian raised his eyebrows in a question, but said nothing.

"I'm serious, Mike. One day I got a phone call. I think the voice was disguised, but he gave me some information that identified him as a senior officer. Information that only someone on Executive Row would know. Then he told me to distance myself from the search for the mole because other people were looking into it. And that was all he would say. Except that I would learn in a few days that I hadn't been sidelined in the force."

"And the second reason."

"It was just like the man told me. A few days later I was made deputy to David Mallory on the Toybreaker case, which meant I was given a big chance to boost my career. If the investigation is successful."

"And why shouldn't it be?"

"Because of David Mallory."

"For God's sake, man, he's one of the finest detectives in the country. He's got more commendations than I've had hot dinners."

"I know he's good, Mike. But this time he thinks he's been set-up."

"And why's that?"

"He's got a personal vendetta with Clayborn."

"That shit. He's an ACC now, I hear."

"That's right. He's running Crime Management, so he's David Mallory's boss. But apparently, there's bad blood between them and Clayborn's just waiting for the chance to get David taken off the case in disgrace."

"Ah, I see the picture. If David Mallory goes down, Chief Inspector Falcon goes down with him. That's the way you're thinking, is it?"

"Well, let's face it, with all the backlash over the mole, it wouldn't take much to sink the ship."

O'Brian nodded. "Too true. So there's only one sure and certain way out of this mess."

"And what's that?"

"Leave it to the man at the top to take care of the mole problem, while you and David Mallory make sure the Toybreaker investigation doesn't fail. Go and get the bugger."

CHAPTER 12

The first subject to come up at the evening meeting was the attack on the paedophile.

"I'm surprised it's taken so long to break out," Mallory said. "This city's been on the edge for too long."

"Will it increase the pressure on you people?" Hannah asked.

"For sure, it will." It was Falcon who answered. "As if things weren't bad enough without the mob rearing its ugly head."

"So let's move on." Mallory turned to Hannah. "Do you have the preliminary profile for us yet?"

"Yes, I put it together last night." She projected her notes onto a wall screen for them to study.

After a few moments Mallory broke the silence. "How far forward does this take us?"

"We know now that the Toybreaker is a woman, and the eyes in the preservative and the nurse's uniform, together with the chloroform and the fibres found at the crime scenes all suggest she has a medical connection."

"True, but we'd already exhausted that line of enquiry. So what can this profile tell us that we didn't already know?" It was interrogative, a policeman's question that cut straight to the chase: why were they bothering with a profile at all?

But Hannah was ready for him. "I think the value of the profile lies in the 'speculation' section. In a nutshell, the profile suggests we're looking at a woman who has suffered some kind of trauma. A trauma that was serious enough to act as a trigger and force her to become the Toybreaker and abduct the children. And she appears to present as being more and more angry with time. All of which suggests that we're looking at someone who's going to up the stakes and commit even more hideous crimes. Because she won't care any longer."

Falcon nodded. "I'll buy that. So how do you suggest we use the profile?"

"I think we should home in on the possibility that the Toybreaker's lost a child, or is close to someone who has. For a start, prepare a new database of all parents and immediate family associates of every young child that has died in the Garton area within the past twelve months."

"What age range?"

"To begin with, use a cut-off at five years old."

"Do you want it limited to suspicious circumstances only, or is it to cover all child deaths."

"All deaths. If, and at this stage it is a big if, the Toybreaker is acting in anger as a result of the loss of a child it need not necessarily be reported as a suspicious death. It might be due to a road accident or to what the Toybreaker might considers medical negligence. So we cover all child deaths."

"Fair enough. But what do you mean by immediate family?"

"That's more difficult to define, I agree. It may be that the Toybreaker herself isn't a parent, but I can see the difficulty in trying to compile a comprehensive list of all immediate family for every death. So as well as the parents confine it to siblings and grandparents for now.

"And then what? How do we use the database?" Mallory seemed content to let her lead. For the moment.

"We cross check with the other databases held in the system. What we're looking for ideally is a nurse, or someone associated with the medical profession in another way, or a social worker, who has recently lost a child. Or is close to someone who's lost a child. Probably, but not necessarily, in suspicious circumstances." Hannah hesitated then.

"And?" Mallory prompted her.

"And I still believe the Toybreaker has a history. But I suggest we leave that for a while."

Before they could carry on the discussion a WPC knocked on the door of the office and came in.

"Sir," she spoke to Mallory. "There's someone at the desk who claims he can help with the Toybreaker investigation. DI Clark spoke to him, and he said to tell you we may have a breakthrough at last."

CHAPTER 13

Mallory was waiting with Hannah in an interview room in the Operations Centre. It was a small cubicle containing a table and four chairs and a trolley with a tape recorder on it.

"I'd like to be present at the interview," Hannah said. "But is it allowed?"

"Yes. He'll only be giving a witness statement and he hasn't been arrested or charged. So he's not under caution and there's no problem with you being there. Unless he objects, of course."

There was a knock on the door and Falcon came into the room followed by a man in his mid-thirties. He was well-groomed and wore a designer track suit and expensive trainers. Falcon led him to a chair and waited until he'd sat down.

"Mr Devril, you came here voluntarily and you are free to leave at any time. You won't be cautioned, but we would like this interview to be recorded. Do you have a problem with any of that?"

"None at all, chief inspector." He voice was middle class, relaxed.

Falcon walked over to the tape recorder and broke open a pack of tapes. He placed two in the machine, and switched it on.

"The Toybreaker Investigation. Witness statement from Mr John Devril on the eighth of December. Time, 21.15. Present, Chief Superintendent Mallory, Chief Inspector Falcon and Dr Hannah Nightingale, a clinical psychiatrist on the staff of the Waring special hospital."

Falcon came back to the table and sat opposite John Devril. Hannah and Mallory sat at either end facing each other.

Falcon looked at a piece of paper that had been given him by the officer on the front desk, and read from it. "You are John Devril of Moor's Cottage, Orchard Lane, Garton?"

"Yes."

"You came forward to the police voluntarily as a witness?"

"Yes."

Falcon was being very careful, knowing that any evidence could be discounted later if it was felt that everything had not been made crystal clear at the start of the interview.

"Mr Devril, would you please confirm for the tape that you do not wish to be legally represented."

The question seemed to shake him, as if he had never considered that he might need a lawyer there.

"Is it necessary? For me to be legally represented, I mean?"

"That is entirely up to you. I don't know the nature of anything you might disclose as the interview proceeds, or whether it might be self-incriminating, but it is sometimes prudent to have a lawyer present even when information is given voluntarily, as it is in your case."

"No, it's all right." Devril seemed to regain his composure. "I don't need a lawyer."

"Just one other point, Mr Devril. Dr Nightingale is a clinical psychiatrist who is employed by the police on the Toybreaker investigation. We would like her to be present throughout this interview and to ask questions if she sees fit to do so. Do we have your permission for this?"

"Yes, I just want to make a statement."

Falcon smiled. "Sorry if all that seemed a bit formal, but we have to follow procedures. I'm sure you understand."

"Of course."

"Now, what is it you wish to tell us?" Falcon settled back in his chair.

"I'm a geologist in the oil industry and I've been working abroad, in Nigeria, for the past eight months. I got back two days ago and today I saw an article in the local paper about the Toybreaker. The article was a follow up to the mob attack on the paedophile and it was the first I'd heard of the case, although I understand it's been creating quite a stir over the last few months."

"You could say that," Falcon agreed. "And you think you have information that could help us?"

Devril hesitated, suddenly unsure of himself. "This Toybreaker, he's been snatching children. Children that have never been found. Right?"

"That's what the Toybreaker does." Falcon was calm and patient, not wanting to force the pace. And Hannah noticed that he didn't contradict when Devril referred to the Toybreaker as male.

Devril sighed. "I've got two young kids of my own, and I can't even begin to think of what it must feel like if they'd been taken away."

"Neither can I, Mr Devril." Falcon sensed a conflict in the witness and wanted to empathise with him. "But I've seen the suffering of the mothers first hand and, believe me, it's a terrible thing. What the Toybreaker's doing is inhuman. Absolutely inhuman."

"Yes." Devril seemed to come to decision, and the words came flooding out. "It's the clowns, you see. There was a picture of one of them in the newspaper article, and I recognised it. It was one of a set my brother made. I think he may be the Toybreaker."

CHAPTER 14

Falcon glanced at Mallory, a flicker of excitement in his eyes. But when he spoke there was an iron control in his voice. As if he was reluctant to allow even a trace of optimism to surface after the long months of bitter disappointment.

"Tell us about your brother."

"Peter has always been what people called 'simple.' It could have had something to do with his birth and the supply of oxygen to his brain, but the doctors were never sure."

"What's his IQ, Mr Devril?" Hannah asked.

"I'm not sure, but I know he was diagnosed as having a mild learning disability."

"Is the fact that a person has some degree of learning disability always apparent?" Falcon pushed the point, wanting the technicalities to be as clear as possible right from the start.

"To some extent it's always apparent, yes," Hannah replied. "But up to a point it can be hidden by verbal ability. In other words, by the ability of a person to express their views and understand instructions."

"Thank you." Falcon turned back to John Devril. "Sorry about that, I just wanted to understand your brother's condition."

"That's all right. The family had problems understanding Peter's condition as well. But the point I want to make is that he wasn't . . ." Devril groped for the right word, "He wasn't the village idiot. Some of the time he had enough verbal ability to appear almost normal. It was just that he seemed to view the world with a naïve simplicity. The kind of simplicity — wonder, if you like — that a child has. Only Peter never grew out of it. But there were things he was good at. One of them was woodcarving, and without any formal training he showed an extraordinary skill at it. The doctors said he had a Savant Syndrome."

"Savant Syndrome?" Mallory looked at Hannah Nightingale.

"It's a condition in which people with a variety of developmental disabilities can have islands of ability which show quite stunning levels of achievement. They are out of character and in complete contrast to rest of their handicap."

"And woodcarving of the type used in the clowns, that would fit the pattern?" Mallory asked.

"Oh, yes. Anything artistic. Drawing, sculpture, carving." She turned to John Devril. "Tell me, did the doctors treat Peter by attempting to train the talent?"

"Yes, he attended a special school where he was encouraged to carve in order to increase the level of his social skills. A conduit towards normalisation they called it."

"Mr Devril, can you tell us about the clowns, please?" Falcon was anxious now to steer the conversation away from the finer points of psychology and back to the investigation.

"Of course, but I have to backtrack a bit first. The teachers at the school recognised Peter's ability and when he left they got him a place on a collage carpentry course for students with learning disabilities. When he was there he developed a speciality in toy making, beautiful hand-carved toys they were, and later the college placed him in regular employment with Days Long Ago, a non-profit making organisation that runs carnivals, art festivals and firework displays for schools and local councils."

"What exactly did he do at Days Long Ago?"

"It was ideal for Peter because he could use his artistic skills and get paid at the same time. As part of their carnival service they ran puppet displays, and Peter used to do all the maintenance on the puppets, repainting them and so on, and even making new ones when they were needed. Then later, the puppeteer taught him how to work the dolls. In fact, he became so good that they let him do one or two spots in shows on his own. But it was the kind of organisation where everyone mucked in and he learned a lot of other skills too."

"And he was able to lead a normal life outside work?" Mallory pushed the point.

"Oh, yes. As I said, he was a bit simple and there was some degree of mental impairment, but he could cope with most things in his own way. Even so, my parents worried that his simplicity would make him vulnerable in society. Which was why they were so glad when he met Carol at a youth festival that Days Long Ago organised. She was a nurse, a paediatric health visitor, and she saw something in Peter that most people missed."

There was a slight pause there and Falcon, an experienced interviewer, picked it up.

"You say your parents were glad when he met this girl. You didn't share their enthusiasm?"

"I always thought there was something odd about her."

"Odd, in what way odd?

"I suspected she was a religious fanatic. I say suspected because it wasn't obvious, and she didn't seem to belong to any of the cults or sects. Or even go to church, come to that. It was just the odd thing she used to say from time to time."

"What kind of thing?"

"Oh, I don't know. Like something was a 'terrible sin' and would 'bring down the wrath of the Lord.' Stuff like that. And she used to quote from the Bible a lot. Anyway, Carol and my brother were married a few months after they met and they bought a Victorian terraced house in a derelict area of the city, cheap because it was on the fringes of a run-down council estate."

"How old was your brother when he got married?" Mallory asked.

"Twenty-two. And I must admit it was a good marriage, at least to begin with. Peter worshipped her and he told me they were happy in a way he'd never believed possible."

"You said it was a good marriage to begin with. Did things start to go wrong later?" Hannah followed up on his remark.

"Yes. It was after the baby was born. I was never sure exactly what happened because Peter was reluctant to talk about it. On the surface it seemed as if they grew even closer together as a tight-knit family group. The baby, it was a boy they called Jason, became the centre of their lives and the three of them seemed to turn their backs on the world."

"Not unusual with a first baby," Hannah said.

"No, it's not. It was the same when we had our first. But with Peter it was different. It seemed to go farther than just being a happy self-contained family. For one thing, Jason never seemed to have any friends to play with, and even when he started at school his parents kept him apart. To the extent that they used to have his birthday parties just for the three of them."

"Did all this strike you as being strange?"

"Yes, and after a while I began to suspect that Carol felt a kind of jealousy towards the boy. It was almost as if she resented him coming between her and Peter, and as Jason grew older I think she felt she was losing control of the situation."

"How do you mean, losing control of the situation?" Hannah leaned forward in her seat.

"Carol was the strong personality in the relationship and to be honest Peter was easy to dominate. But it was more than just dominating him. She had to be in control. I remember once suggesting that Peter should do something that Carol didn't entirely support, and the change in her was frightening. Her eyes seemed to cloud over with a kind of rage. She fought it down, but I saw it."

"And you think it got worse after the baby was born?"

"I'm sure it did. Before the baby she could control Peter, but later he became so attached to the boy that her power over him diminished."

"And this worried you?"

"Yes, it did, but I began to think I was imagining things because most of the time Carol was the perfect mother. And Peter was absolutely devoted to the boy, and he seemed so happy. Except . . ." He hesitated. "Except that there were hints he dropped from time to time, and I began to suspect that Carol was reasserting her control in other ways. More sinister ways."

Mallory started to say something but Hannah held up her hand.

"What kind of sinister ways?"

"I think she was violent to him."

"To Peter? You mean, he was a battered husband?"

"I'm still not sure, but I think so."

"And did this urge of Carol's to be in control again take any other forms?"

"Peter talked about sins he and Jason had committed and the punishments they both had to suffer for them. He wouldn't go into details, but I got the impression that they involved things that were abnormal." His voice faltered. "Christ, I should have done something to stop it." He was sobbing now.

"Look would you like a break for a few minutes?" Hannah asked him. "Perhaps a cup of tea?"

"Yes. Just a few minutes."

"I'll get someone to take care of it." Falcon went over to the tape recorder.

"Interview suspended at 21.55 at the request of Mr Devril who requires a break."

He turned the machine off and led Devril from the room.

* * *

"Sorry about shutting you up just now, David. But once he'd mentioned that he thought his brother's wife was playing control games I wanted his thoughts to stay focussed."

"No problem. You're the expert, but before he comes back there's one thing I'd like to get clear in my mind."

"Just one?"

"For now, yes."

"And what's that?" Hannah was curious to see the way his mind was working.

"Peter Devril is one of these, what was the word, savants. I don't understand yet what the full implications of that are, but it seems to me that it's his wife Carol who's the fruitcake here."

"I agree, that it's Carol Devril who appears to be the *fruitcake*, as you put it. And she also seems to fit the profile of the kidnapper. Or most of it. But there's one critical characteristic missing so far, and that's a personal trauma involving children. She must be on the database for nurses, but the new database listing dead children's not ready yet. So we can't cross match. Even so, on the basis of the information we have so far, particularly her access to the wooden clowns, I'd say she's a prime suspect for the Toybreaker."

But that conclusion was to be shattered in the next few minutes.

* * *

Falcon turned the tape recorder back on and dictated the formal interview identification procedure. Then he walked to the table and sat down facing the witness.

"Mr Devril, do you feel able to continue?"

"Yes, I'm all right now. I just needed some time."

"Good, so tell us about the clowns."

"Peter had always made toys for the boy, and they became more elaborate over the years. The family had few friends, but when a new neighbour moved in next door they became close to her. She was a primary school teacher who lived alone, an Australian, I think. Anyway, when she saw some of the toys that Peter had made she told him they were good enough to sell and suggested he tried to market them at craft fairs. Peter was enthusiastic about the idea and he made a first batch of eight, personally designed, wooden toy puppets in the form of clowns. To test market reaction the clowns varied in size from six inches high to a full life-size toy as big as a small child. He had a workshop in the basement of the house and he made the clowns in secret. So that he could surprise Jason when they were finished. He often did that, it was a kind of ritual between him and the boy. He kept the clowns in a locked steel cupboard, but he left it open one day and Jason saw them. Peter was out and Jason showed them to me, but made me promise I wouldn't say anything to his dad. The clowns were beautifully carved and very distinctive, and that was why I recognised one of them in the article about the Toybreaker."

"And as far as you are aware, no one else knew about the clowns?"

"Apart from the next door neighbour, and presumably Carol, no. And the neighbour's back in Australia now. Which is why the clowns wouldn't have been recognised by anyone else from the photographs in the papers."

"So on the evidence of the clowns left at the crime scenes, you think that either your brother, or his wife Carol, is connected to the Toybreaker?" Falcon asked the question almost casually.

There was no answer and the silence in the room dragged out.

"Mr Devril?"

"It can't be Carol." The words were forced out of him.

"Why not?"

"Because she's dead."

CHAPTER 15

"How did she die?"

John Devril looked up, and it took an obvious effort for him to drag his mind back. "For years the council estate close to where they lived had been on the decline, and many of the tenants in the houses had left. Those remaining formed a hard core, a rump of socially deprived no-hopers, and the streets became a battleground for vandalism, stolen car racing and drug dealing. In the end, the problems became so bad that the council decided to demolish the entire estate and build one of those new inner-city 'villages' that are all the rage now. Once the plans were made public a local builder saw the opportunity of putting up a shopping mall to service the new development. But to do that he needed to buy up the houses in the row where Peter lived. The terms offered were good and all the occupants agreed to an immediate sale and left their houses. Except Peter and the girl living next door, and she was only delaying a sale for a few months until she went back to Australia. But Peter was adamant. He wanted to stay in their own little house, and Carol backed him up. In fact, she seemed even more determined to stay than he was."

"So, apart from the girl, your brother and his family were the only ones defying the builder?" Falcon edged him along.

"Yes, and that's when things started to turn nasty. The builder employed a local security firm, ostensibly to keep vandals off the properties that had already been vacated. But in reality their job was to persuade Peter to sell up. When they failed they turned to strong arm tactics and one evening a petrol bomb was thrown into the house. The police believed that it was only meant to frighten the family, and it was unlikely that it would have started a major fire. But unfortunately Peter had bought three cans of paint stripper to clean the wooden floor in the hall and had left them by the door. They acted as an accelerant and the fire spread rapidly. Peter was out at the time, and when the fire brigade broke into the house they found the bodies of Carol and Jason on the upstairs landing. The fire hadn't reached that far, but they'd both died from smoke inhalation as they'd tried to escape the blaze. So that's why Carol can have nothing to do with the Toybreaker. She died in the fire."

"Where had Peter been?"

"He said he had a headache and needed to walk it off in the fresh air. But . . ."

"But what?" Falcon let him take his time now.

"When I talked to him the day after the fire, he seemed a bit reluctant to talk about where he'd been. But I expect it was because he was feeling the shock. Anyway, by the time he got back the firemen had already entered the house."

"What was the date of the fire?" Mallory asked.

Devril thought for a moment. "Sometime in August this year. The twenty-third, I think."

"Was anyone arrested for starting the fire?"

"Yes, two men were charged and the trial is coming up soon I think."

"And what happened to your brother? After the fire, I mean?"

"He disappeared. Dropped out of sight completely. Even the police couldn't find him, and they needed his evidence in the case against the men who started the fire."

"Thank you for coming forward, Mr Devril. We have your address and we may need to speak to you again at a later time. For now, I'm going to offer you a choice of the tapes used for recording the interview. Then I would like you to make a written copy of your statement and sign it. A WPC will assist you with the formalities."

CHAPTER 16

"Christ." Falcon shook his head. "Our first major breakthrough. And now we find out the prime suspect's dead. I thought it was too good to be true."

They were in Mallory's office, drinking coffee, and they'd just listened to the tape of the interview with Devril.

"There's something not quite right here," Mallory sounded worried. "I can't put my finger on it, but my copper's instinct tells me Carol Devril's too good a suspect just to drop out of the picture."

"I feel the same thing." Hannah was glad that Mallory had been the first to bring it up. "I said before that she fitted the profile. So just let me run it past you again. *Number One*, she's a woman. *Number Two*, her husband made the clowns. *Number Three*, she's a nurse, which gives us the medical connection. *Number Four*, she's a health visitor, which gives her access to single-parent family records. *Number Five*, she appears to be a religious fanatic. *Number six*, she's a control freak, which is a characteristic of many serial killers. *Number Seven*, she would have suffered a trauma when her son was killed in a fire. The trigger event. In the preliminary profile I called it the most important part of the equation because it could solve the paradox of why the Toybreaker should have to fight an internal battle between good and evil."

"How does the fire solve it?" Mallory was caught up in her argument.

"Before I answer that, can you pull up the dates of the abductions?"

"Sure." Mallory switched on his computer, tapped in his password and watched the menu list unfold. Then he opened one of the files and a list appeared on the screen.

"OK, when did John Devril say the fire at the house occurred?" Hannah asked.

"The twenty-third of August," Falcon answered.

Hannah looked at the dates on the screen. "Bingo. The date of the fire in which Jason Devril died fell between crimes two and three. Just before the Toybreaker started to leave a lock of hair at the crime scene.

"Am I missing something here?" Falcon asked.

"Look, there's no doubt the Toybreaker arranged each crime scene very carefully," Hannah explained. "And it was done so that a smashed clown, and sometimes a lock of hair, was placed on view. But there was a progression in the way the lock of hair was presented to the mother. When it first appeared, it was placed on the pillow. Later, it was thrown on the floor, and finally it was sent through the post. Although we haven't had anything from abduction number six yet."

"So?" Falcon still sounded mystified.

"What I didn't understand was why there was no lock of hair left behind at the first two crime scenes. But we know now there was something different about those first two abductions. They took place *before* the fire occurred. That's what was different about them."

"Sorry, I still don't understand."

"I think Carol Devril showed compassion after the first two crimes because she'd lost a child herself. But it didn't stop her abducting children, and the evil side of her personality was gradually taking over again. In other words, leaving the lock of hair was no more than a transitory phenomenon. I tell you, Carol Devril fits the Toybreaker profile in every respect. Every single one."

"But she's dead." Falcon looked at the two of them and shook his head. "She died in the same fire that killed her son. All this about her changing after the second abduction doesn't stand up because she was already dead before the third crime took place."

"But don't forget, a woman dressed in a nurse's uniform was seen leaving the last crime scene," Hannah interrupted.

"That still doesn't alter the fact that Carol Devril's dead. I'm as disappointed as you are, but unless there's been some kind of resurrection, she's out of the frame. Tough shit, but end of story. We should be concentrating on the husband, Peter Devril."

"You're right," Mallory agreed. "Finding him is top priority. So for starters, see if his brother's got an up-to-date photograph of him then get on to the press office. All media and police forces to be issued with the photograph and notified that we want to talk to Peter Devril in connection with one of several lines of inquiry we're actively pursuing. Stress that no one should approach him, but should report all sightings to the police. The usual crap."

"Will the media buy that?" Falcon sounded dubious.

"No, but we need their help and it might stop some of the wilder speculation."

"OK, I'll go along with search for Peter Devril," Hannah agreed. "For one thing, you don't have any choice now you know about the clowns. But bear with me, please. At the same time I'd like you to run a series of checks on Carol Devril. Everything you can get on her background over say the last ten years. And we need to extend the 'dead child' database, push that back to cover the last ten years as well. I want to be able to cross match it with her activities as a nurse."

"Why?" Falcon didn't seem convinced.

"Baggage," Mallory muttered the word, the sound almost inaudible.

"Baggage?" Falcon echoed.

"Hannah believes the Toybreaker has a history. That whoever it is comes complete with baggage." He turned to her. "That right?"

"Yes," Hannah hesitated. "But I don't really want to face the kind of baggage we might be dealing with here. Not yet anyway."

CHAPTER 17

The curtains were open and the stars were crisp in the winter sky which hung like a mantle over the black river.

Hannah put the gin and tonic on an ornately carved coffee table, kicked off her shoes and sat down on the sofa with a sigh. She had just come back from a party after the opening of the new exhibition at the municipal art gallery and she was tired. She had gone in place of her grandmother, who had felt unwell.

She sipped her drink and thought about her grandmother. The Nightingales had been an important family in Garton for over two hundred years. The family shipping business had been sold off after the Second World War but the Nightingales had retained their reputation as great social reformers, merchant philanthropists who were fervent believers in the welfare state and who had played a prominent role in the development of the city as Garton entered the twentieth century.

Hannah's grandmother, Charlotte Nightingale, was an independent thinker and had been one of the first women to graduate in Social Science from Garton University. She became part of the family after she married John

Nightingale. He was a local MP and as well as helping him in his work, Charlotte had served for years on the local council and on various bodies that struggled to obtain better conditions for women and children in the city. But she had a great sense of family, a belief in the position of the Nightingales in the city, and she had carried on with her community work after her husband died.

They had one son, Phillip. He married late in life, but it had been a love match and Hannah's recollections of her early childhood were of a happy close family. Life was comfortable and happy, but when she was six both her parents were killed in a car crash.

Hannah would never forget that day. She'd been brought to the family mansion, where her grandmother had been waiting for her. Charlotte Nightingale was a legend, a martinet who was forever propounding the Victorian virtues of the family. An imposing, and if truth be told, a rather frightening figure. At least that was the way she appeared to a six-year-old girl. And when Hannah saw her standing in front of the fireplace in the drawing room that day she immediately burst into tears.

In a panic she'd fought to stop the flood of tears, thinking for some reason that her grandmother would be angry with her for showing weakness. But then a strange thing happened, and instead of being angry the formidable woman rushed across the carpet, threw her arms around the little girl, and began to cry herself. That was the start of the deep bond that grew between them.

From the beginning Hannah had been brought up to be a Nightingale. Even as a young child she had accompanied her grandmother to civic functions, learning her role as a Nightingale. As she grew up she'd been encouraged to make her own decisions, to follow the path of an independent young woman. But the groundwork had been laid. Very carefully laid, Hannah realised later. She'd attended the best local schools and had read medicine at Edinburgh. But first and foremost she'd been brought up to believe she was Hannah Nightingale, a member of a family with status in the city. And even now, after she'd returned to Garton as a clinical psychiatrist with a growing international reputation in her field her grandmother still expected her to fulfil a social role in the city, something they talked about during their regular Sunday lunches.

At first, Hannah had quite enjoyed the role of a society woman, but as pressures of work grew she began to resent the time it took. And particularly the effect it had on her love life. Or would have done if she had a love life, she thought ruefully, and not for the first time recently she found herself thinking about that side of her life. In a vague kind of way she was aware of time passing and she didn't need Charlotte's gentle reminders that she would like to see great grandchildren before she was too old to appreciate them, to remind her that her biological clock was steadily ticking away.

But then her thoughts would drift to Craig. Wonderful, warm hearted, handsome, clever Craig.

She'd first met him at the start of her appointment at Deacon Gauter's clinic in the States. A colleague, one of the senior researchers at the clinic, was holding an end of summer barbecue at a rented beach house on the New England coast, and a crowd from the university had gone along. Hannah had been introduced to this tall, rangy ex-US Marine with blond hair and blue eyes, wearing jeans and a faded cotton shirt. For a few minutes they'd stood there talking, and after that they hadn't left each other's side during the rest of the evening.

It had been the start of a wonderful year. Craig had a post teaching English Literature. He loved the rapport with his students and was one of the most popular members of the faculty. But his great ambition was to be a writer, and he already had a successful book of short stories published. The stories were based on his experiences in the Marines, and the volume had received strong critical acclaim.

Within weeks of their first meeting, Hannah had moved into his place, a small brownstone house in a terrace close to the campus. She would never forget that golden fall, caught in her mind in a kaleidoscope of sepia-coloured memories. Short misty days and long evenings spent around open fires; deep, animated student discussions of literature and the universe and the meaning of life; pasta bathed in delicate herb sauces, bread drizzled with olive oil and grilled on forks, wine rich and red; the sense of wonder in the discovery of language as the tapestry of the novel Craig was writing unfolded; the huge pine bed with the heavy duvet that used to fall onto the floor during the passion of their love making. And always, through everything, the two of them. Locked together until they seemed to be one single entity.

Until that night. That terrible night when Craig went out jogging and never returned. Attacked by a junkie on a footpath in the woods fringing the campus. Robbed and left to die in the cold.

There had been other men since then, of course. But none of them had lasted and as she sat, staring out into the crisp darkness of the night, Hannah wondered if she still judged all men against the memory of her lost love. She found the idea of being locked into that kind of time trap oddly depressing, and she sighed again. Then her mobile rang, shattering the mournful train of thought.

She retrieved the phone from her handbag and took the call. It was Falcon and he wanted her at the Operations Centre straight away.

Bloody Hell, she thought, This is becoming a habit. Hoping to delay the visit until next morning she muttered something about having had too much to drink. But Falcon was insistent and said he'd send a police car round to pick her up.

When she asked him what had happened, he said that the data on Carol Devril had come in.

And he sounded scared. Really scared.

CHAPTER 18

There were pools of darkness in the Operations Centre as Hannah walked through, but one or two operators were still sitting in front of their computer screens and there was a background hum from a power generator.

Falcon was waiting in his office. It was on the platform next to Mallory's but it was an even smaller cubicle, with barely enough room for the desk, which had a computer on it, and two plastic chairs. As Hannah came in Falcon took her coat and waved her to seat in front of the desk.

"Sorry to drag you out so late in the evening." His voice sounded oddly distracted.

"Where's the chief super?" Hannah asked him.

"He'll be here in a few minutes."

"So what's important enough to keep me from my beauty sleep?" she asked.

He'd been holding his breath and he expelled it with a sharp explosive sound. Then he turned to face her and for the first time she saw the expression in his eyes. Fear. Like he'd seen a ghost.

"Some things it's best not to know." His voice was so low she could hardly catch the words.

She was surprised. "You don't mean that. Not in a police investigation."

He looked at her. "No, I don't, do I? We're not allowed to turn away. It's part of the job description. Never mind the things we see, it's . . ." He was interrupted as Mallory came into the office.

"Evening." Mallory nodded to Hannah, then turned to Falcon. "So what have we got, Gary?" He placed his jacket on the back of a chair.

"Deep shit, guv. The deepest. I'll show you."

They crowded around the desk. "More data came in this evening," Falcon said. "I've now put everything in one master file and you can both have a copy. But I'll run through the salient points now."

He pulled a printout from a file on the desk and studied it for a moment.

"We've run a full check on Carol Devril using every source we could and we can put together a picture now. She was white, twenty-eight years old, born in Nottingham and married to Peter Devril. She was trained as a paediatric nurse and worked in Garton as a health visitor for an agency that supplied nurses to health centres. She didn't appear to have many close friends, and people who worked with her at the agency described her as varying from 'cold and stand-offish' to 'shy and difficult to get close to.' She wasn't very forthcoming to anyone about her private life and never joined in socially with the other nurses. Same sort of pattern emerged from colleagues at the health centres where she worked."

"Almost a classic type." Hannah nodded. "An anti-social loner who didn't go in for close relationships."

"But there was one exception. She lived in a flat in the Seatown area of Garton, and apparently she became quite close to a girl living in one of the other flats." Falcon looked at the printout. "A Mary Connelly, who was a secretary with a legal firm in the city. The two of them used to go out together, to films and clubs, that sort of thing. But the strange thing was Carol dropped Connelly as soon as she met Peter Devril. And I mean dropped her. Like a lead brick. Connelly wasn't invited to the wedding and she told our people that she never even met Peter. She was very hurt about the way she'd been treated."

"I can understand that," Hannah said. "But what was her overall impression of Carol before the break-up?"

"She said she thought Carol was bragging a lot of the time. Always making up stories about her rich family and golden childhood, and how important her job was. As if she was after attention."

"Low self-esteem." Hannah nodded. "Anything else?"

"Apparently, she used to quote from the Bible a lot."

"But have we any indication of what she was like after she'd married?" Hannah asked.

"Not a great deal, no. Apparently, she withdrew further into her shell. But she continued to work and she did talk about the child sometimes."

"What kind of things did she say?"

"The usual, as far as I can tell. How he was sleeping, when he cut his teeth, what kind of toys he played with. The sorts of things young mothers talk about. But again, there was a contradiction here because one day she'd be happy to talk about the kid, but the next day she snap at anyone who asked. In the end, I think her colleagues simply became weary of her, and just didn't bother asking anymore."

"Did she have any close friends during the time she was married?" Mallory asked.

"There was the girl who used to live next door. The teacher from Australia that John Devril mentioned. We can try to track her down if need be."

"Maybe." Mallory shrugged. "But as you said yourself, Carol Devril's dead. So what's the point in pursuing any of this?"

"It's not that simple, I'm afraid," Falcon sounded tired suddenly.

"What do you mean, not that simple?" Mallory had caught something in Falcon's voice.

"We extended the dead children's list back over the period Carol Devril worked here, as Hannah asked." He turned to her. "You said you wanted to be able to look for cross matches between Carol Devril and dead children. Well, I already ran that for you."

"And?" She was afraid to ask the question.

"I think you've already guessed what I found."

"What's going on here?" Mallory looked from one to the other.

"Look." Falcon brought up a new programme on the computer and lists of names and times scrolled down the screen. He tapped a few keys and seven of the names were highlighted.

"It's all there." There was a cold edge to Falcon's voice. "Those young children died over the period. Seven of them. The deaths occurred in different areas of the city but in each of the cases we're looking at the children were all under two years old, came from single-parent families, and were suffering from acute bronchial disorders. And Carol Devril was the paediatric nurse who attended them all. Too many coincidences. Far too many."

"Jesus." Mallory rubbed his hand across his eyes. "We really have found ourselves a serial killer."

"So if the deaths were down to Carol Devril, how did she kill the children?" Hannah asked.

"Don't know." Falcon shook his head. "The deaths were all reported as bronchial disorders."

"But surely, someone would have picked up on this before now," Mallory sounded dubious suddenly, as if he didn't want to believe any of it. "For God's sake, seven young kids died in similar circumstances in the care of the same nurse. Wouldn't that have rung bells, particularly because of all the fuss about cot deaths?"

"Not necessarily." Hannah shook her head. "Let's look at those similar circumstances you mentioned. For one thing, Carol Devril was an agency nurse, which meant she worked for a number of health practices, not just one. So why should anyone cross match the deaths in the first place? But more important, we have to look at the *manner* of the deaths. You referred to cot deaths, and you're right, there is a lot of attention focussed on those. But the whole point is that a cot death, or sudden infant death syndrome, is suspicious. Or at least unexpected. But all these kids were suffering acute bronchial illness and the deaths themselves wouldn't have been considered either unexpected or suspicious."

"But there would have been post-mortems, wouldn't there?" Mallory still didn't sound convinced.

"You can check, but I doubt it. A doctor will only report deaths like these to the coroner if the parent directly requests it, or if the death itself is suspicious. Like cot deaths are. But these weren't suspicious because the children were already suffering acute bronchial problems And don't forget, the deaths happened over a period of years. Put everything together and we've got different health practices, different locations, and a long time span."

"So she could have got away with it?" Mallory was visibly shaken.

"Yes. Except for one thing."

"And what's that?"

"The Toybreaker appeared on the scene, and we started turning over the stones."

CHAPTER 19

Falcon was late when they met for the daily briefing the next morning.

"Sorry, dental appointment," he said as he came into Mallory's office, his voice slurred from the anaesthetic in his gums

"Right, we've all had time to think about this now." Mallory waved Falcon to a chair. "So let's look at what we've got. There's no doubt, at least not in my mind, that Carol Devril was a serial killer. We'll pass the information along, and that's going to open up a whole new can of worms But Carol Devril's dead, so how does her past impact on our investigation?" He turned to Hannah.

"It's a very different ball game now. A mentally disadvantaged man with savant tendencies married to a serial killer. From a professional point of view it's a fascinating combination. Uncharted territory. But to answer your question, David, I simply don't know how it impacts on the Toybreaker case. But I do think we need to complete the picture, or as much of it as we can, because we have to know more about both Carol and Peter Devril. Especially about their life together."

"So what are you suggesting?" Falcon forced the words out, grimacing at the pain.

"Two things to start with. First, we locate the next door neighbour, the teacher that went back to Australia, then interview her. Either by phone or email, or whatever, but she's the only person who appears to have been close to the Devrils after they were married. Except for Peter's brother John, of course. So second, we interview him again and this time we probe deeper into the personal relationships of John and Carol Devril."

"If you'll excuse me I'll get started." Falcon stood up. "When I've taken a full bottle of aspirin, that is."

"I'm still not sure where we're going with this?" Mallory said when Falcon had gone out.

"And neither am I." Hannah couldn't reassure him. "It's uncharted territory."

* * *

When Falcon came back into the office he looked worried, Hannah thought. But she couldn't tell if was something to do with the investigation, or the result of the pain in his mouth.

"I contacted John Devril again, and I've arranged for him to come in for another interview this afternoon?"

"Did he seem happy to cooperate?"

"Very happy. I think he still feels guilty that he didn't do something about the way Carol was behaving before it was too late. I also asked him for the name of the girl living next door. He only knew her first name, Wendy, but he remembered the name of the school where she taught. So I phoned the secretary to get Wendy's address in Australia." He hesitated then, unsure of himself.

"And?" Mallory prompted him.

"You're not going to like this, guv. The secretary told me that the police in Australia were in touch with the school a couple of months after Wendy left. Apparently, she never showed up, and her parents reported her missing. One of the teachers at the school here in Garton, a Janet Gaskill, was particularly friendly with her and has been in contact with her parents over the past few months. Apparently, Wendy still hasn't surfaced, and nobody's heard a word from her."

"When was she expected to leave Garton?" Mallory sounded as if he didn't want to ask the question.

"On the day of the fire at the Devrils' home." Falcon looked across the desk at Mallory. "Who identified the bodies at the house?"

"It'll be in the file I got from the fire brigade." Mallory opened a drawer in the desk and pulled out a file. He shuffled through the papers inside, then snapped his fingers. "Here it is. It was Peter Devril. He identified the bodies.

"Were there any DNA tests?" Hannah asked.

"No." Mallory shook his head. "There was no need for DNA, or a check with the dental records either. Carol Devril and the boy died from smoke inhalation and the bodies weren't badly burned. No one questioned Peter Devril's identification. Why should they?"

Mallory was silent for a few moments, tapping the fingers of his right hand on the desk. Something was there at the back of his mind. A feeling familiar from hundreds of investigations. A feeling that he was about to make a breakthrough.

"Here." He opened the file on the fire investigation and shuffled through the contents, pulling out a photograph. "These are the two bodies, and you can see the faces clearly."

"Can I look?" Hannah held out her hand and Mallory passed her the photograph. For a moment she studied the face of the woman. But there was no clue there as to whether it was the face of a serial killer. But that didn't surprise Hannah. She was only too well aware that serial killers live in the community and don't exactly advertise their calling. Then she looked at the face of the boy and saw only an innocent child.

"So let's have that teacher, the one who was friendly with the Australian girl, to take a look at the photo. Get her here as soon as you can, Gary."

* * *

As it turned out that the teacher had a free period and Falcon sent a car around to collect her. Mallory, Falcon and Hannah waited for her in one of the interview rooms

"Miss Gaskill." When she came in Mallory introduced the people in the room. "Thank you very much for coming here at such short notice."

"No problem." She was young, in her mid-twenties, a pretty girl dressed in a white blouse and dark skirt. "I've been so worried about Wendy ever since she went missing."

There was something in her voice, Hannah thought. An edge of desperation, perhaps. Was Wendy just a friend, or was there more to it?

"Miss Gaskill, we think you may have important information regarding an investigation we're carrying out, and if you've no objection we'd like to make this a formal interview. We'd also like to have Dr Nightingale present."

Janet Gaskill looked surprised, but shook her head. "I've no objection."

Mallory signalled to Falcon who walked over to the tape recorder and went through the procedure of inserting fresh tapes. Then he switched the machine on.

"The Toybreaker Investigation. Witness statement from Janet Gaskill on the tenth of December. Time, 10.15. Present, Chief Superintendent Mallory, Chief Inspector Falcon and Dr Hannah Nightingale, a clinical psychiatrist on the staff of the Waring special hospital."

They all sat around the central table and Falcon began the interview.

"You are Janet Gaskill, and you're a teacher at Marybank School, Garton?"

"Yes, I am."

"And you were a friend of Wendy Sanderly, an Australian teacher who recently worked at the school?"

"Yes."

"A close friend?"

"What do you mean?" Her head snapped up suddenly.

Falcon was surprised at her reaction. "I meant only that you knew her well. That's all."

"Sorry, I'm a bit on edge. Yes, I knew her well."

"OK, I'm going to show you something." He looked at Mallory who passed him a glossy black-and-white print. "For the tape, I'm showing Miss Gaskill a photograph, TB Evidence Exhibit 32, taken by a scene-of-crime officer investigating a fire at the home of Peter and Carol Devril." He placed the print on the table. "Miss Gaskill, can you recognise anyone in the photograph?"

For a moment there was silence in the room as they all stared at the photograph. Then Janet Gaskill leaned forward and traced her finger across it.

"Oh, God, it's Wendy."

"Are you sure?" Falcon wanted firm conformation.

"Oh, yes, I'm sure. She's even wearing the necklace I gave her. You see, we were lovers." She looked at them defiantly. "Yes, lovers and I was going to join her in Australia." Suddenly the dam broke and she burst into tears.

Hannah heard Mallory's voice, too low to be caught on the tape. But she heard it.

"Christ. Carol Devril's still alive."

Hannah remembered the words of the banner headline in the *Evening News.*

EVIL IS WALKING THE STREETS OF THE CITY.

CHAPTER 20

"In the light of all this new evidence, I think we can assume now that Carol Devril is the Toybreaker," Mallory said. "And believe me I've been waiting a long time for a break like this. But there's still one very important question to be answered. Peter Devril identified one of the bodies found in the house as that of his wife. So why did he want everyone to think she was dead? Does it mean Peter and Carol Devril are running the Toybreaker together? Hannah?"

"I don't know. Both of them, Peter and Carol, are complex characters. And then there's the young boy to consider. What effect did his death have on them? Particularly Peter, since his brother said he worshipped the boy. I'll have to give this some thought, but I'll try and come up with something for the next briefing."

Mallory accepted that. "So first things first. We have to find the Devrils. Top priority. All the stops out. And we've already started the search for Peter Devril." He turned to Falcon. "Can you give us an update on what's come in so far?"

"The public have reported several possible sightings around the city, although none have been confirmed yet.

But we have been able to put together some background information on him. In response to the photograph we circulated, a PC in Furley, a town about twenty miles from Garton, recognised Devril as a man he'd picked in the town centre on a date which turned out to be three days after the fire at the house. Devril was wandering round lost and he appeared to be distressed, so the PC took him to the station. Once he saw the state the man was in, the duty sergeant called in the FME who admitted Devril to the Symond Clinic, a local mental health unit, as a voluntary patient. But he discharged himself two weeks later. We also know that three days after that he drew a sum of five hundred and eighty-five pounds out of the bank. That was the total balance left in a joint account he and his wife used to have their salaries paid into. He's not been back to work since the fire, but he hasn't approached the bank for a loan either."

"Right. So now we enlarge the media search to include his wife. God knows, the two of them must be holed up somewhere. Although five hundred and eighty-five pounds won't go far."

"I'll need another photograph — of Carol Devril this time," Falcon said.

"Try John Devril, he's probably got photos of his brother's wedding."

"I'll get onto it straight away." Falcon left the office, and Mallory turned to Hannah.

"Can you check with the clinic where Devril spent those two weeks. It might give us something useful."

* * *

The report came in as just as Falcon was about to call it a day and go home.

It was from one of the officers on the Garton force. He'd been off sick and had only returned to duty that evening, and it was the first time he'd seen the photograph of Peter Devril. Apparently, eight days before he'd been called to a suspicious death among the vagrant community in a derelict area by the docks. It finally turned out that the death was due to natural causes, but the PC remembered seeing a man among the down and outs who fitted the photograph.

Falcon called Mallory straight away. Then he set up a team and arranged for the officer who'd sent in the report to accompany them to the docks.

It was dark by the time they reached the derelict area. It was a place of shadows, and thin tendrils of mist drifted across the patches of open ground. The team moved forward across a surface of compacted clay, stumbling over the bricks and lengths of old timber scattered around. The smell of the river, dank with slime, carried from the black stretch of water dimly visible between the shells of the tall warehouses looming through the murk. And something else was on the air. A mixture of foetid bodies and oily smoke.

Figures were clustered around a fire burning in a metal drum, shapes that moved in the dancing flames. They were dressed in an odd mixture of old clothes and some held bottles in the hands. But they all seemed indifferent, as if it was a normal part of their life, as the police moved among them checking faces.

"Not here, sir." The PC who'd reported seeing Peter Devril in the area walked over to Falcon.

"Any point in questioning them?" Falcon nodded towards the shadows around the fire.

"One maybe," the PC said. "He helped with the body last time. I'll bring him over."

He returned with a small thin man dressed in an old army greatcoat that fell to his heels.

Falcon grimaced at the smell and shone a torch onto a photograph of Peter Devril. "We're looking for this man, have you seen him around here lately?"

The PC held out his hand with a banknote in it, careful to shield the gesture from prying eyes.

"No, I haven't seen him. Now piss off and leave us alone." The man pocketed the note in a single movement. "Over there by the edge of the old warehouse. Got a patch of his own." The words were whispered as the man stamped away.

Falcon didn't approach the warehouse straight away, not wanting to brand the tramp as a nark,' and instead he moved the police in a broad sweep across the area. They finished up against the outer edge of the warehouse building. The wall around it had been partly demolished and two of the police team stepped through a gap and stopped by the rusted metal frame of a window on the ground floor of the building.

To the side of them a brick outhouse was standing against the wall. There was a heavy wooden door in the end facing the policemen and one them pushed it open and shone his torch inside. Then he called out and the rest of the team formed a semi-circle around the door, leaving a gap for Falcon as he came forward.

Inside the outhouse someone had made a crude attempt to provide a living space; a sleeping bag on the floor, a primus stove and some cooking utensils on a wooden shelf, and an old metal-frame canvas chair against one wall. A photograph of a young boy in a metal frame was standing on an orange crate.

A figure was rising from the sleeping bag, rubbing his eyes, and Falcon looked at his face in the light from the torches.

They'd found Peter Devril.

CHAPTER 21

"You're absolutely certain," Hannah asked. "There was no sign of Carol Devril?"

"None. Peter Devril had been living in that hut on his own," Falcon replied. "No doubt about that. None at all."

They were in Mallory's office, waiting for the duty solicitor and the FME to arrive.

"So it doesn't look as if they're working this together." Hannah paused for a moment, thinking. "Strange. Very strange, since Peter Devril obviously lied to make it look as if his wife was dead. What reason would he have for doing that if he wasn't in it with her, I wonder?"

"Maybe it'll come out during the interview," Mallory said.

"About the interview." Hannah looked from one to the other. "We have to be very careful. Following your request, I contacted the Symond Clinic and got a preliminary report from the responsible medical officer who treated Peter Devril. Once I'd explained that he was wanted in connection with the Toybreaker abductions, the RMO was willing to bend the medical confidentiality rules. Up to a point anyway. When he was admitted, Devril was diagnosed as suffering from temporary amnesia. He appeared to recover from that, but he was depressed and totally uncooperative. He also showed signs of paranoia, which became acute when he was asked questions about his background. It got bad enough for the RMO to consider putting him on a section, which would have allowed them to keep him at the unit. But then Devril disappeared. Make no mistake about it, though, this is a fragile personality. Very fragile. Which means that he could break down, and maybe even recess, at any point in the interview if the pressure on him gets too much. And I'm sure none of us wants that."

"No, we don't," Mallory agreed. "For one thing we can't afford for his brief to start yelling that we're using excessive pressure on a vulnerable individual. This has to be by the book. But, as you say, Devril *is* vulnerable, and we can't just treat this as the interview of an ordinary suspect. We have to walk on egg shells."

"True," Falcon agreed. "But at the end we still have to come out with something concrete to charge him with."

"It's bloody mess." Mallory sighed. "But let's just run through the procedure. As I said, the last thing we want is to make any mistakes here, and the main point to consider is Peter Devril's mental state. As the senior police officer present I have a duty of care to formally advise Devril's brief that I have a *suspicion* that his client might be suffering from a mental impairment. The grounds being the information provided by his brother and what Hannah's just told us about his stay in the Symond Clinic. It's still only a suspicion, but if the FME gives consent to go ahead with the interview the brief must be advised that because of his impairment his client's in a vulnerable condition and has the right to have an appropriate adult present during the interview. I'm sure the brief knows that anyway, but I'm simply making certain we come out of this squeaky clean. Then if everything is cleared, we go ahead with the interview knowing that we covered all the bases."

"Which still leaves us with the problem of how to proceed with the interview," Falcon pushed the point.

"Agreed." Mallory thought for a moment. "Let's look at this. We arrested Peter Devril on suspicion of being involved in the abduction of young children. The evidence being that he made the clowns found at all the crime scenes. Even if he denies making them, we've got his brother's interview on tape. So we've got enough to charge him. Problem is, he might just have a perfectly plausible explanation for the clowns turning up like that. Maybe they've been stolen or something. Which could mean that if nothing else comes out at the interview, Devril could walk. So what else do we have on him?"

"There's only one other possibility," Falcon said. "Charge him with making a false statement to the investigating authorities about the death of his wife in the fire."

Mallory shook his head. "A serious offence, I agree, but his brief could claim it was simply a mistake under circumstances of great stress, particularly for someone suffering a degree of mental retardation, and Devril would probably get bail anyway. So he'll still walk."

"Which will not be good." Falcon sighed. "He's the first real break we've had in the case. We can't just let him go and risk losing all contact with the guy. But, as you said, we have to get it absolutely watertight. So," he turned to Hannah, "we'd appreciate your advice on how to go about questioning Devril."

For the next twenty minutes Hannah coached them in how to approach the interview. While that was happening the duty solicitor and the FME arrived. They spoke with Peter Devril, and both agreed the formal police interview could go ahead. When it started Hannah watched proceedings through a two-way mirror.

Falcon opened a fresh pack of tapes and placed two of them inside the recorder.

"The Toybreaker Investigation. Police Interview with Peter Devril on the eleventh of October. Time, 22.16. Present, Peter Devril and his legal representative Miles Willthorpe, Chief Superintendent Mallory, and Detective Chief Inspector Falcon. Peter Devril was arrested at 20.15 hours today on suspicion of being involved in the abduction of young children. He was cautioned at the time of the arrest by DCI Falcon, the arresting officer."

While Falcon was going through the procedure Hannah studied Peter Devril.

The police had obviously provided him with a fresh set of clothes, and he was wearing jeans and an open neck blue denim shirt. And he must have washed, because he looked reasonably clean. He hadn't shaved and his face was dark with stubble. But it only looked like a single day's growth, so he'd apparently been taking some care of his appearance. Except that he'd let his hair grow, and it fell around his shoulders in long untidy streaks.

She looked at his face. He seemed older than mid-twenties but that could easily be the result of living rough, she thought. The features of his face were ordinary, with nothing to distinguish him from the crowd. Except for his eyes. They were bright blue, and seemed almost too large for the rest of his face. Sensitive eyes that were in contrast to the rest of his appearance.

"For the record, before we begin I would like to confirm two points with Mr Willthorpe," Falcon said. "Firstly, your client has been seen by the FME who declared him fit to be interviewed and you agreed with that decision?"

"Yes, after speaking with him myself I won't contest the decision that my client is fit to be interviewed."

"Second, you waived the right for your client to have a responsible adult present at the interview. Will you please confirm that?"

"Yes, I confirm it. However, I have pointed out his rights to my client, and stressed that he does not have answer any question he doesn't want to. And, if the need arises, I shall advise him of that right as the interview proceeds."

"Thank you, I am familiar with the correct interview procedures." Falcon understood what was happening. Willthorpe was covering his back, and the chief inspector wasn't in the least fazed by the lawyer's attitude.

He turned to Devril. "You are Peter Devril, currently of no fixed abode," Falcon started the interview.

"Yes." He was staring down at the table top, avoiding looking at them. And he spoke in a low voice.

"Do you know why you have been arrested, Peter?"

"Yes, for harming little children."

"And have you harmed any children?"

"No, I like little children."

"Peter, I understand that you used to live at," he consulted a sheet of paper on the table in front of him. "Fifteen Rose Croft Villas, Garton."

"Yes." A monosyllabic reply, the tone neutral.

Mentally, Falcon ran through the three basic principles Hannah had set down as a framework for questioning Devril.

One: try to establish a rapport with him so he'll start to believe he's safe. Two: approach important topics slowly by stealth, not head on. In that way, he won't recognise them as being important. Three: if there's something he obviously holds back on don't threaten him by forcing the issue there and then. Instead, move onto other topics then come back to the stumbling block. That way, there's every chance the barrier will eventually fall.

"Mr Devril, tell me a bit about yourself. How old are you?"

"Twenty-eight." Still no eye contact.

"Where were you born?"

"In Garton."

"Did you go to school in Garton?"

"Yes."

It was like talking to a machine, Falcon thought.

"Did you like it at school?"

"Like it?" The first sign of interest in a question. "I liked it better when I went to a special school. They didn't pick on me there."

"Did other children used to pick on you a lot?"

"Some did. But my brother always stuck up for me."

An opening here, Falcon thought. Time to start probing. But remember, come at the question from the side. "When you were at this special school was there a particular activity you liked best?"

"Yes, I liked woodwork." For the first time he looked up. "I was good at it."

"And what sort of things did you make?"

"You know, shelves and cabinets. And toys. I liked making the toys best of all."

"Did you carry on making toys when you left school?"

"Yes, I had a workshop at home."

"Did you make the toys for your little boy?"

It was there then. A sudden change of body language. A sag of the shoulders as his head fell forward. And when he looked up there were tears running down his face.

"He's dead. We did things together but Jason's gone away now. He was so small . . ." The tears came faster now and his nose was running.

"Chief Inspector, I think we should take a break now," Willthorpe cut in. "This line of questioning is obviously upsetting my client."

"Would you like a drink of water?" Falcon spoke directly to Devril. He was reluctant to take a break, knowing that he'd have to start building up the rapport all over again when they restarted.

"Thank you." Devril accepted the glass of water Falcon poured for him from a jug on the table, and drank it all down.

"Here." Falcon passed over a handkerchief.

Devril took it and wiped his face. He gasped for air as the sobs subsided, but he seemed to be recovering.

"Can we proceed?" Falcon looked at Willthorpe.

"Is that all right with you, Peter?" The solicitor asked Devril. "You don't mind more questions?"

"Don't want to talk about Jason. Don't want to." There was a stubborn edge to his voice now. Like a defiant child.

"OK, Peter, we'll move on," Falcon reassured him. "When you left school did you get a job?"

"Yes, I worked at Days Long Ago," he said proudly.

"And what did you do there?"

"I helped to set up the displays. I used to like that. Especially the fireworks. But best of all, I did woodwork. Making screens and panels for the displays. And I used to make puppets. Then later on the man who operated the puppets showed me how to work them. And when I was good enough he let me have a small spot in his act."

"Did you enjoy working there?"

"Yes. It was nice."

"Did you ever tell them that you made toys yourself in your workshop at home? Wooden toys?"

"No. They were just playthings."

"Were the puppets just playthings?"

Peter Devril's head snapped forward suddenly and a look of something appeared in his eyes. Fear, Hannah thought. Or something else. Cunning perhaps.

Falcon picked up on it at once. "What was special about the puppets you made, Peter?"

There was a long drawn-out silence and Peter Devril seemed to shrink inside himself.

Falcon let the silence run, then in a sudden movement he reached down and lifted a plastic bag from beneath the table. He put it down in front of Devril. Inside was the crudely reconstructed remains of a brightly painted wooden clown.

"Is this one? Is this one of your clown puppets, Peter?"

"Damn, you shouldn't have done that. Too confrontational," Hannah spoke out loud as she watched with horror through the glass.

Peter Devril's body jerked upright and his mouth was dragged open in a wide gash. Then he screamed.

And the terrible power of that scream seemed to echo off the walls of the room.

CHAPTER 22

They had to wait until Peter Devril had calmed down before they could decide how to proceed, and they left him with a WPC who gave him a cup of tea. Mallory, Falcon and Willthorpe went to the chief superintendent's office where Hannah joined them.

Willthorpe insisted that his client was unfit to be interviewed any further that evening, and Mallory had to agree.

But they were still faced with the problem of Peter Devril's health. The police had the right to detain him overnight without charge, but there was no way they wanted someone in his mental state held in police cells. And for the same reason Willthorpe agreed that they couldn't simply release him to go back to that hovel on the docks.

"Could we have him sectioned?" Falcon asked. "That way he can be detained in a secure unit."

Hannah shook her head. "His mental state is frail, but there's no grounds to section him. Although I agree that keeping him here is completely out of the question. If he breaks down he'll need specialist staff to handle him."

"So what do we do then?" Mallory sounded frustrated.

"There is one possibility," Hannah said. "Let him stay at Cascade House."

"What's Cascade House?" Willthorpe asked.

"It's a halfway house for patients with mental disorders who are to be released back into the community. I could arrange for them to take Peter Devril in and look after him until he's fit to be interviewed again. The main point being that he will have expert care at hand if his condition deteriorates."

Willthorpe agreed but Mallory asked to speak to Hannah in private, and they went out of the room.

"This Cascade House, is it secure?" Mallory asked.

"No, but there are trained staff in attendance around the clock. They can't force Devril to stay, but at least they can inform us if he leaves."

"How long does Devril need to recover?"

"Difficult to say, but at least overnight. We can review the situation again then."

"If we want to appear whiter than white, I think he needs longer. Say a good twenty-four hours."

"What are you up to, David?"

"I've just remembered. Cascade House is on Jenkins Drive, isn't it?"

Hannah nodded. "Yes. It's a modern purpose-built unit."

"Surrounded by a tall brick wall topped with razor wire?"

"Yes, but it's a rough area and the precautions are to keep intruders out, not to keep the patients in."

"But the only entrance is a pair of wooden doors in the outer wall?"

"That's right."

"So we can keep the place under surveillance and put a tail on Devril if he leaves the unit."

"Put a tail on him? You mean you'd let him roam around free?" Hannah sounded surprised.

"I certainly would. But if he does, he'll be followed closely and every single move he makes will be known to us."

"But why do you want him free?"

"Because he might just lead us to Carol Devril."

"You mean you're planning to use him to spring a trap?

"You could put it like that, yes." He grinned. "But don't tell Willthorpe."

* * *

Hannah had a full list of patients at her clinic in the special hospital the following day, but she was free to attend a briefing at the Operations Centre in the early evening.

"Thanks for coming in, I know you've had a busy day," Mallory greeted Hannah as she came his office.

"Tell me about it." She sighed as she dropped into one of the plastic chairs.

Mallory nodded sympathetically. "We'll take you for a drink later, after I've brought you up to speed."

"Is there much to catch up on?"

"Two things. First, I sent a scene-of-crime unit to the Devril house."

"So what did they find?"

"According to the report they sent in, nothing that could help us. Apart from the fact that it was half burnt-out, it appeared to be a normal family home."

"And the second thing?"

"I thought you'd like to know how Peter Devril spent the day."

"He left the unit?"

"Yes, at about half past two in the afternoon. We had a team watching the building and Devril was followed. He waited for a bus at the top of the road and went to the area where he used to live. Then he walked to the family house. At that stage I brought in a mobile unit that was on standby. I kept the unit out of sight, but I took over command on the ground."

"Did Peter Devril try to go inside the house?"

"No, apparently it's all boarded up. But from his reaction, the men on his tail said just seeing the place seemed to upset him."

"What made them think that?"

"It was his general body language. According to one of the officers, he seemed to slump inside himself when he saw the place where he used to live. And he seemed to be crying."

"So what did he do then?"

"He went into a corner shop at the end of the next road. When he came out he was carrying a plastic bag. He went back to his house and crossed the road to a grass slope that falls away towards the docks. There's a path of sorts there, and Devril followed it to about halfway down the hill then turned off into a small thicket of shrubs against a brick wall. One of the men tailing him stayed at the top of the hill where he had a good view of the whole slope, and another approached the thicket. He radioed in to the mobile unit then reporting that he could hear Devril talking, and he thought he'd arranged to meet someone there."

"Carol Devril?" Hannah looked up sharply.

"That's what I thought. That we'd sprung the trap, and I flooded the area with officers. There was no way Carol Devril could have escaped the net."

"So what happened?"

"Nothing." Mallory sighed. "There was no one else in the thicket. Just Devril. And his memories."

"His memories?"

"That's right, the poor sod was back in the past. Apparently, from what one of the officers learned later when he interviewed the woman who runs the corner shop, the thicket was a special place where Devril used to take his young son for picnics. That was why he'd gone to the shop. He bought a bottle of lemonade, two packets of crisps and two Kit Kats. Exactly the things he'd bought when the boy was alive."

"So Devril was reliving the happy times he had with the boy?"

"That seems to be it." There was an edge of sadness to Mallory's voice.

So the tough in-your-face policeman had a soft spot, Hannah thought. An empathy with a man who was obviously suffering the loss of his son.

"And Peter Devril was talking to himself?" she said.

"That's right. Or, no, I suppose strictly that's not right. He was talking to the boy."

"So what happened then?"

"Nothing. Peter Devril let the officers take him back to Cascade House. Meek as a lamb."

Falcon came in then and the three of them went out for the drink Mallory had promised.

CHAPTER 23

"The Toybreaker Investigation. Police Interview with Peter Devril resumed on the thirteenth of October. Time 10.34. Present, Peter Devril and his legal representative Miles Willthorpe, Chief Superintendent Mallory, and Chief Inspector Falcon."

"Peter, are you happy to answer some more questions?" Falcon asked.

"I suppose." He kept his eyes downcast.

"Do you like the place where you're staying now?"

"It's all right. I've got my own room."

"And what about the food, is it good?"

"Not really." He made a face. "It's a bit like being back at school."

Falcon smiled. "I know what you mean. It's the same in the canteen here. What's your favourite food?"

"Jason liked egg, chips and beans. I like that too."

There was no sign of agitation when he mentioned the boy's name this time, so Falcon decided to crank the interview up a notch or two.

"Peter, you went out yesterday. Where did you go?"

"I went back to where we used to live." Still no eye contact.

"You went back to see your old house. But there had been a fire there hadn't there? Can you tell us what happened?

"My wife and little son. They died." Still no sign of emotion. It was as if his mind was somewhere else.

"You identified their bodies, didn't you?"

"Yes, the police took me to this place."

"The mortuary?"

"The mortuary, yes. I saw the bodies there."

"Chief Inspector, can you tell me where this line of questioning is leading?" Willthorpe came in. "What has it to do with your present investigation?"

"I'm not sure yet," Falcon replied. Devril hadn't appeared shaken when he'd talked about identifying his wife's body. In fact, he hadn't shown any sign emotion at all since he'd come into the room. So he decided to change the topic. "Mr Devril, where did you go after the fire?"

"A home. A place where they looked after me."

"Why did you leave the home?"

"Because the doctors kept asking me questions. They wouldn't leave me alone."

"Didn't you like the questions?"

"No." His voice was raised for the first time. "I didn't want to talk about it."

"What was it you didn't want to talk about, Peter?" Falcon's voice changed, cajoling now he thought he was getting through at last.

Silence. Drawn out until it seemed to fill the air.

"What didn't you want to talk about?" The same question again. Gentle but insistent.

There was a sudden change in Peter Devril. An abrupt tension that seemed to run through his entire frame. His fists clenched and his shoulders became rigid.

"The fire. When they asked me why I was wandering the streets I told them about the fire. But they kept asking for details. Going on and on at me."

He was shaking now and his voice was becoming fainter as he fought with his memories. Falcon knew that if he pursued that line of questioning there was very little time left before either Devril lost it completely, or his solicitor stopped the interview. So he switched direction. But he had no idea he was moving into even deeper water.

"Peter, let's go back to what we were discussing at the end of the last interview. The wooden clowns you made. What happened to them?"

"Carol took them away."

"Why did she do that?"

"She needed them?"

"Why did she need them, Peter?" Falcon was patient, letting Peter Devril set the pace. But his reply was totally unexpected.

"BECAUSE OF WHAT SHE WAS DOING." The words were screamed out, shocking the people around the table.

"And what was she doing?" Still the soft voice from Falcon.

"She was the Toybreaker. She killed little children."

There. It was out in the open at last. The first confirmed identification of the Toybreaker.

"How did you know Carol was the Toybreaker?"

"She told me."

Amazingly, Peter Devril seemed to have calmed down. As if admitting that his wife was the Toybreaker had released the strain he'd been under, and Falcon decided to make the most of it.

"Why did she tell you?"

"To punish me. Me and Jason. Because she said we were drifting away from her."

"But was her being the Toybreaker a punishment for you?"

"She made it look as if I was involved because of the clowns. She showed me the pictures of them in the paper, and said unless I did what she said she'd tell the police that

I was the Toybreaker. And she said they'd believe her not me, because I was retarded."

His voice was starting to wander again now, and there was one vitally important question Falcon still had to ask. He knew he was taking a chance, but he needed to return to the fire.

"Peter, we've seen the photographs taken after the fire at your house. Why did you say Carol was dead when you knew she wasn't?"

"Don't know. Haven't seen her since the day of the fire." His voice had become truculent, almost aggressive.

"Where is she? Where's Carol now?" Falcon forced the issue.

"Told you. Don't know." The voice was slurred and words seemed to be dragged out of him this time.

Falcon realised there was no point in proceeding any further at that stage and with the agreement of Willthorpe he terminated the interview. As they left the room he gave the solicitor the choice of tapes from the recorder.

* * *

"What did you make of all that?" Mallory asked Hannah when they were back in the chief superintendent's office. "We've got an ID on the Toybreaker. It confirms what we suspected, but how much weight can we put on Peter Devril's evidence?"

"Not a lot, I suspect. A good lawyer would tear it to pieces. But we have learned one thing."

"Which is?"

"The incredible the lengths that woman was prepared to go to in order to maintain control over Peter Devril. To the extent of threatening to expose him as the Toybreaker. God, how she must have made him suffer."

"Anything else show up?" Mallory asked.

"I'm not sure at the moment. I want to study the tape in more detail before I draw any conclusions. That's all right, isn't it? With Devril back at Cascade House, I mean."

"Yes, I'd rather have a considered opinion than a knee-jerk reaction. So take your time." He sounded depressed.

"Wait a minute, let's be positive here," Falcon tried to sound upbeat. "OK, Peter Devril's evidence might not stand up in court, but it reinforces our belief that Carol Devril's the Toybreaker is. So let's up the tempo of the search for her. We've just got to be careful how we handle it. We don't want it generally known that we actually suspect her of being the Toybreaker, or God knows what would happen to her if she's found by a member of the public. No, we just have to stress how urgent it is that we interview her in connection with the investigation. Hammer it home. And use every modern technique we can get our hands on. Make certain she has no place to hide. It's all we can do for the moment, but she'll be found. In this age of technology and CCTV there's just no place for her to hide in the end."

But Falcon was wrong. There *was* one place she could hide.

CHAPTER 24

The next day was Saturday and Mallory said they'd earned a chance to relax, and he took them for a pub lunch in the village where he lived, a small place nestling in the hills outside Garton. The pub seemed to be a genuine old-fashioned, coaching house. A log fire was burning in a huge fireplace in the lounge, and they sat around a small table by the side of it.

"You feel it sharpens the mind to get away from headquarters?" Hannah asked Mallory.

"No." Falcon shook his head. "He just likes the beer."

Mallory grinned, but he didn't contradict his colleague. Then he became serious. "My copper's instinct tell me something's wrong with this case."

He took a drink from his glass, and put it back down on the table. Then he reviewed the case. Succinctly, point by point. When he'd finished he sat back. "So what's wrong? What are we missing?"

"OK, I don't know if we're missing anything. But one thing does bother me." Falcon shook his head. "The search for Carol Devril is one of the most intense national exercises ever carried out by the police. I doubt there's a single person in the whole UK who doesn't know Carol

Devril's face by now. But there hasn't been a single reliable recent sighting of the woman. Not one."

"But surely there's nothing unusual in that? She'll have seen all the publicity and she'll have gone to ground, won't she?" Hannah made the point.

"Yes."

"So what's the problem?"

"The problem is, no one has reported seeing her for the last six months. Not since the fire at the house, in fact. That's what really puzzles me. No one can just disappear like that without trace."

"Not unless they want to." Hannah refused to be put off.

"What do you mean?" Mallory was suddenly alert.

"I said, not unless they want to. Look, David, maybe we've been approaching this from the wrong angle."

"Go on." Mallory was watching her closely now.

"You're both worried because the search hasn't thrown up any sign of the woman. Not at this moment, because she'd be expected to go into hiding as soon as she knew the search for her was on, but in the immediate past. Which I agree is strange. Unless she'd *already* gone into hiding. And has stayed in hiding for the last six months."

"But why cut herself off completely?" Mallory was still probing.

"Jesus, the mask," Falcon snapped out the words. "We didn't pay enough attention to the mask. We just assumed that it was part of the nurse's get-up."

"So." Mallory still couldn't see where this was going.

"So, we know now that Carol Devril didn't die in the fire. But suppose she'd suffered burns. Burns to her face. That could account for why she was wearing the mask."

"And it could also account for the fact that she went into hiding after the fire." Mallory nodded.

"Exactly. We'll have to check the hospital A & E units to see if anyone came in for burns treatment around that time. But if we assume for the moment that she cut herself off from society, someone must have been looking after her. Buying food, that sort of thing."

"And more than likely that someone is her husband. Peter Devril." Mallory snapped his fingers. "But wait a minute, he's been living rough down by the docks and we know she wasn't there with him."

"All right," Hannah cut in. "But maybe she didn't want him living with her, not if her face was badly scarred. I know I'd want to be alone if it happened to me."

"But he could have kept her in the necessities," Mallory agreed. "I think it's likely Peter Devril's been sheltering his wife. Which means he's in this deeper than we thought. A lot deeper."

"You think he knows where Carol Devril is?" Hannah asked.

"I'm beginning to think he does."

They had lunch and tossed some other ideas around, then Mallory invited them back for coffee. He lived in an end house in a terrace of red brick Victorian cottages, and he drove the car round the side and parked on a track at the edge of a long garden.

Hannah knew that David Mallory was divorced, and she was intrigued to see where he lived. When she got out of the car, she looked over the low fence surrounding the garden. At first glance, the garden seemed a jumbled mixture of styles, but on closer inspection the theme of the design became apparent. Individual garden rooms were arranged in a linear sequence, with a curving central lawn running through them like a path. At intervals, points of interest had been added, a small statue here or a pillar with an urn on top there, to lead the eye forward along the path.

"Hobby of mine." Mallory waved his hand across the garden. "Got to have something to keep you sane in this job. But it's been a bit neglected this year, what with one bloody thing and another."

The front garden of the cottage was tiny, a checkerboard path of terracotta and black tiles fringing a patch of lawn behind a low wall topped with iron railings. Mallory unlocked the door, pushed it open and ushered them inside.

Hannah had wondered what the house would be like. Now, as she came into the hall, the first thing that struck her was that David Mallory was untidy. But it was a comfortable untidiness, with outdoor clothes and footwear scattered around a tall stand. The second thing struck her when she entered the living room. This was a strictly masculine house. The furniture was old pine and had obviously been carefully selected but the way it was arranged, and the mixed colours of the curtains and covers, totally lacked any design sense.

A fire had been left burning in the black leaded cast-iron grate, and as they entered the room an enormous dog stood up, shook itself, and moved to Falcon. It was a German Shepherd and it obviously knew Falcon and allowed him to pat its long hair. Then it turned to Hannah.

"Is he friendly?" she asked, standing quite still.

"Not usually. He's been trained to be suspicious of strangers, and . . ." Mallory's voice trailed off as the dog wagged his tail and began to lick Hannah's hand.

"Well, that's the first time he's taken to anyone straight away."

"He's just a big softie, aren't you?" Hannah scratched him behind the ears.

They were not exactly the words Mallory would have used to describe the animal, but he let it go.

"How long have had him?" she asked.

Mallory grinned. "A couple of years. He sort of adopted me. He was retired from duty as a police dog when he broke his leg. His handler couldn't keep him and he brought him into the station one day to see if anyone else wanted him. I left to go out to the car and the brute followed and jumped inside. And that was it. Now I'll put the coffee on. You two make yourselves at home."

Hannah looked around, realising how little she knew of David Mallory outside of work. On either side of the fireplace the wall space was taken up by floor-to-ceiling shelves crammed with a books and Hannah walked over to look at them, believing that you tell a lot about a person from what was on their bookshelves.

They ranged from thrillers to volumes on various sports, with a scattering of classics.

But what really caught her eye were the photographs on a small round table under the window. The one at the back, in a plain wooden frame, was a black-and-white image. Taken on a dark winter's day, it showed a man in rugby kit with an expression of extreme physical strain on his dirt streaked face. He was clutching a ball to his chest and was handing off an opponent as he moved through a sea of mud towards the try line ahead. It was a stark study, in which the photographer had somehow caught an image of raw power, and it took her a moment to realise the subject was David Mallory. Next to it was a larger team photograph, in colour this time. The players were wearing jerseys with primrose and blue hoops, and were grouped around Mallory who was holding a large cup. There was an inscription under the photograph which read: *Garton Rugby League Club. Winners Excelsior Challenge Cup Final. Wembley.*

The photograph at the front of the display showed an attractive young woman grinning mischievously at the camera as she posed in mortar board and gown.

"My daughter, Karen." Mallory saw Hannah looking at the photograph as he brought the coffee in on a tray. "Taken on her graduation day when she qualified as a dentist."

"You must be proud of her."

"Very proud."

He put the tray down.

"And this one." She indicated the black-and-white photograph.

"That won a journalistic award. It was on the cover of a Sunday supplement when they did a feature on rugby league. Apparently, it captured the grit of the game."

"And you played for Garton?"

"A long time ago. I was loose forward in the cup-winning side."

"And captain?"

"And captain."

"When did you finish playing?"

"Two years later. I was carrying a knee injury and the doctors said it could get worse. And since that could have finished my career in the police, I retired from the game. But no regrets. I had a good run."

"Indeed he did," Falcon said. "He's far too modest to say, but he captained Great Britain on tour in Australia."

Before Mallory could say anything in reply, his mobile rang. He took it from his pocket.

"David Mallory." He listened in silence for what seemed a long time. "Thanks, I'll be in touch."

"Peter Devril's left the unit, and he's slipped through the surveillance we put in place. He's out there on his own."

"And we now believe he's in contact with Carol Devril." Falcon's voice had a hard edge to it. "Which makes him a very dangerous man. Very dangerous indeed."

CHAPTER 25

They went straight back to headquarters and Hannah and Falcon waited in Mallory's office while the superintendent talked to the officers who'd lost Peter Devril. He returned looking tired.

"How did he get away?" Hannah asked. "I thought he was under surveillance."

"He was. He left Cascade House early in the evening and went back to the road where he used to live. He was followed as he crossed onto the slope leading down to the river. It was dark and the officers trailing him thought he'd gone into the thicket of shrubs where he'd been before. They waited for a while, but when they finally went in there was no sign of Devril. Apparently, he'd left without them seeing. But it's not as bad as it seems. We've got the area sealed off, and we'll pick him up sooner or later. There's no way he can get through the net."

"So what's top priority now?" Hannah asked.

"Locating Carol Devril," Falcon replied at once.

"So let's be positive. There are a number of unknowns in her behaviour pattern. But at the moment, there's one particular point that might help us."

"And what's that?" Falcon asked.

"When she committed the last crime she was wearing a First World War nurse's uniform. For the moment, never mind *why* she wears it. A more relevant question is, *where* did she get it from?"

"We've already been down that road. As soon as we learned about the uniform. We didn't know at the time that Carol Devril was involved, just that someone had been wearing the uniform," Falcon sounded disappointed, as if he'd expected more from her.

"Take me through it." Hannah was determined not to be put off so easily.

"Well, for one thing we know the uniform didn't come from a shop specialising in theatrical costumes. At least not one here, or in any of the surrounding towns. Because we checked them all out. We also checked with local nursing associations, but there was no help there either. It could have homemade, I suppose."

"Yes, it could," Hannah conceded the point. "In which case, we come up against a brick wall. But there is another possibility. It might have come from an old medical establishment."

"We already checked that as well," Falcon said.

"I see," Hannah tried not to let her frustration show. "What did it throw up?"

"Zilch. We complied a database on all the old medical buildings in the area. Infirmaries, hospitals, clinics, medical centres. The lot. But nothing came up. Nothing at all."

"Can we go over the computer files you used in the search for the old medical buildings?"

"Sure, we can." Falcon looked at Mallory. "Can we use your computer to run it?"

"Of course."

"You want to get us in?"

Mallory sat down behind the desk, booted up the computer and keyed in his password. Then he vacated his chair for Falcon who ran his fingers rapidly over the keys and a series of menus scrolled down the screen.

"This is what we did. We divided the medical establishments into sub-sets, depending on type. We looked at old surgeries, prior to modern health centres, that is. Old service hospitals that treated patients from the First World War, and old children's hospitals. We also included National Health facilities that have only recently been phased out."

Hannah thought for a moment. "We'll concentrate to begin with on the fact the nurse's uniform was a First World War outfit. So call up the old service hospitals first. They should be the most promising."

Falcon clicked the mouse on one of the menus and a column of names, about twenty in all, started to scroll down the page. After each name there was a sequence of letters. Falcon highlighted the letters after the first name and explained.

"These all served in some kind of medical role during the First World War. Each one has been assigned a code based on the kind of facility they offered; full hospital, rest home, that kind of thing, and whether they're still operating, closed down but still there, or demolished."

He ran slowly down the list, but the names meant nothing to Hannah. Then suddenly one of them caught her eye. "Hold it there. St. Anthony's."

Falcon stopped with the name highlighted, while Hannah tried to think what had triggered her interest. She knew about St. Anthony's in a professional capacity, because it had been a Victorian mental institution with a novel patient treatment regime. But she was certain that wasn't why her attention had been drawn to it. Then she remembered.

"You once called up a map of the area where Peter Devril lived. Can you get it again?"

Falcon nodded. "Once I get the coordinates, I can."

"OK, if you could do that, please. And can you also give us a printout of the data on the screen now."

Falcon set the printer running then left the office. When he came back he was carrying a yellow post-it label with a series of numbers on it. He stuck the label to the top of the computer before clearing the data on the screen and bringing up another programme. Then he tapped in the code from the label, and a map unfolded on the screen.

"That's the area and there's the house." He highlighted a crescent-shaped area.

"And there's St. Anthony's hospital." Hannah pointed.

On the edge of an open space on the opposite side of the road to the Devril house there was a large building, with a wall surrounding the grounds. The name printed by the building was *St. Anthony's Old People's Home*. And in the grounds, close up to the wall, was a smaller rectangular building with a symbol for a tower and the letters 'hospt' printed alongside.

"St. Anthony's hospital. I thought I'd seen it the first time we looked at the map."

"One hell of a memory you've got." Falcon sounded impressed.

"Not quite as good as you might think. I know the name of the hospital because it was a mental institution that was quite famous in the history of psychiatry. That's why it must have stuck in my mind."

Falcon picked up the computer printout and ran a finger down the list, then read the code against the name of the hospital. "Sorry to disappoint you. Again. But the place was demolished fifteen years ago. That's why we didn't take it any further."

"When was this map drawn up?" Hannah asked.

Falcon shrugged. "I don't know. But I can find out."

He left the office and came back a few minutes later. "They're based on original large-scale Ordinance Survey maps, with extra details added by our people where necessary. And according to the records, the last major update was two years ago."

"So how come a place that was knocked down fifteen years ago is still there on the map?"

"Good point," Falcon conceded. "But one I can't explain just now on a Saturday night with everywhere closed up."

"Maybe I can," Mallory said. "Find out about St. Anthony's, I mean. I know one of the priests who works in the old people's home. I served on a community liaison committee with him a couple of years back and we got quite friendly. I'll phone him, but I'll need to get the number from the phone book in the general office."

He came back a few minutes later, looking thoughtful. "I've asked Father Michael to come over and talk to us in person. I sent a car for him and he should be here in a few minutes."

"Why do we need to talk to him?" Falcon asked.

"Because from what he said the old hospital building is still there. It was never demolished."

* * *

Father Michael was still wearing his cassock when an officer brought him into Mallory's office. He was a huge man who seemed to tower over Mallory as he shook the chief superintendent's hand.

"David, it's been too long." He turned to Hannah and Falcon. "He's not a bad lad for a Protestant, you know. And he was the finest loose forward ever to play for Garton." His voice had a deep Irish brogue.

"Full of bullshit, as usual." Mallory grinned. "He could charm the backside off any of those donkeys that populate what he has the nerve to call God's Country."

Falcon brought a plastic chair from another office and Father Michael sat down, squeezing his bulk into it with an effort.

"David, you said you needed my help." His voice became serious. "Is it to do with this Toybreaker case? I know you're heading up the investigation?"

"Thanks for coming so soon, Michael. And, yes, it concerns the Toybreaker case."

"Dear God, there are some evil creatures abroad. So how can I help?"

"According to the local council records the hospital building in the grounds of St. Anthony's Old People's Home was demolished years ago. But you just told me it's still there."

"The old asylum. Yes, it's still standing. And there's a story behind that. There was a plan by the diocesan authorities to demolish the old building and put up a new geriatric clinic in its place. Planning permission was obtained, funds were raised, and the demolition work was actually started. Then it was found that the treasurer of the appeal that raised the money had been lining his own pockets. By the time the authorities were on to him he'd left the country and he was never brought to justice. But the plans for the clinic had to be shelved. For good, I'm afraid, and the work was called off when just a few outbuildings had been knocked down. I don't know what happened with the council, but it's my guess that they got their wires crossed and it was recorded as having been demolished. And nobody ever thought to amend the records."

"What was the building used for?" Falcon asked.

"Originally, it was built as an asylum for the insane on the site of an old monastery. The man who endowed it, a Victorian social reformer, was a strong believer in the idea that mental illness was related to an evil that struck the soul. I understand that the treatment offered at the asylum was quite humane in its day, but the place always gave me the creeps. Massive mosaics of the Devil and other assorted demons on the walls. I always thought that if you weren't mad when you went in there you'd soon go off the rails with all that stuff around you. Then as treatment moved on, the asylum was converted to a TB hospital for geriatric patients who needed isolating. But in the First

World War it was taken over as hospital for troops who were badly wounded in the fighting. Soldiers who needed operations. For head wounds, mostly. But what has all this to do with the Toybreaker investigation?"

"I'm not sure," Mallory said. "But we might just have located the Toybreaker's base of operations."

"Dear God." The priest half rose from his chair.

"Michael, what is it?"

"The asylum is fenced off from the rest of grounds, and nobody goes in there these days. But a few months ago one of the old people in the home reported she kept hearing noises coming from the other side of the fence. It was an old lady who suffers from Alzheimer's and the staff at the home just assumed she was hallucinating."

"What sort of noises?" Mallory had to force the question.

"She said they were like the voices of little children in distress."

CHAPTER 26

Hannah waited with Mallory and Falcon under the stand of tall trees that faced the entrance to the building. They all were wearing dark blue flak jackets and baseball caps.

Suddenly Mallory's radio buzzed and he lifted the set to his ear. He listened for a few moments, then flicked the switch to transmit and acknowledged the call.

He turned to Falcon. "There's evidence that someone's been inside recently, but the place is completely clear now." The disappointment in his voice was evident. He'd clung onto the slim hope that the children might still be alive in there, and he had a special paediatric medical team standing by.

"No kids?" Hannah echoed Mallory's disappointment.

"No. The hostage snatch team's withdrawing and the inspector will brief us as soon as he's outside."

A few minutes later a figure appeared out of the darkness and approached Mallory and Falcon. He was wearing flak jacket and baseball cap and carried a Heckler and Koch MP5 sub-machine gun.

"What happened in there, Jim?" Mallory stepped forward.

"We had to force the front door to gain entry, and we found the place was deserted. But there were signs that someone had been in there not too long ago. Scraps of food and papers lying around. But our orders were very specific. Check for personnel but touch nothing unless absolutely necessary. Leave that to the scene-of-crime unit."

"Thanks, Jim. Stand your men down. The scene-of-crime unit will take over now."

They waited around in the cold until the scene-of-crime unit had completed their initial survey, and taken all the photographs they wanted. Then the technician in charge, Arthur Fielding, reported to Mallory.

"Three lines of evidence point to recent occupation." Fielding kept his report concise. "One, bits of food and some files left open in an office. Two, possible blood stains, again recent, found in the old operating theatre. Three, signs that a patch of ground enclosed by the cloisters has been recently disturbed."

"Let's go." Mallory tried not to think about the implications of the blood stains and the disturbed ground, but a feeling was growing in his gut.

"Here." Fielding passed Mallory a plastic bag. "Can you change into these, please."

Mallory took one of the white cover suits, a pair of overshoes, and latex gloves from the bag and passed it round. When the three of them were kitted out, Fielding led them to the front door of the asylum. The heavy wooden door was open and they moved through into an entrance hall, brightly illuminated now by the generator-powered searchlights set up by the scene-of-crime unit officers. At the far end of the hall there was a central marble staircase, with an ornate cast-iron banister. On each side of the staircase carved wooden doors were set into the wall.

"Hell," Falcon swore as he looked around, caught by the sheer evil tension of the mosaics on the walls and domed ceiling. They were all around them. Darkly coloured images of Satan and his hordes, viewed through the mass of cobwebs that hung suspended from the ceiling.

"Father Michael was right," Mallory muttered. "They *are* enough to drive any sane person over the edge." He looked at Hannah. "So why have them in this place?"

"The man who endowed the clinic believed in the shock drama therapy for the treatment of the mentally ill. He wasn't alone in that, only in this case it took a religious form. Which is why all the mosaics here portray the struggle between good and evil."

"Bloody creepy, if you ask me," Falcon muttered under his breath.

The asylum building had two floors but according to Fielding there was no evidence that anyone had recently been on the upper level, and he confined the tour to the ground floor. They crossed the marble floor and as Fielding opened one of the doors on the far side a draught of cold air flooded in. More lights had been rigged up here and they could see that they were in a stone flagged passage. On one side there was a row of doors set into the wall and on the other side a series of arched cloisters faced an open space.

All the doors were open but Fielding explained that they'd found nothing in any of the rooms, except for the one at the far end. A light had been rigged up inside, and the room appeared to have been some kind of office once. A row of filing cabinets took up most of one wall, and there was a desk and chair in the centre of the floor. Two white-suited technicians were standing by the side of the desk, ready to bag any evidence once the scene had been examined.

"There, on the desk." Fielding pointed. "That stack of red plastic files. They weren't left when the building was closed. For one thing there's no dust on them, and for another that type of file's fairly new. But we haven't opened any of them yet."

"Anything else?" Falcon asked. He and Mallory were still at the door, looking into the room, with Hannah behind them.

"Not that we can see. Except for a few scraps of food. The filing cabinets are empty, and so is the desk. Whoever used this room apparently just kept the files here. Oh, and one more thing, there's a tape by the files."

"I'd like a copy of that as soon as possible," Hannah said.

"No problem, I'll have one made as soon as we've checked it for evidence."

"Not much is it?" Falcon sounded puzzled. "If this was the Toybreaker's base I would expect more signs of occupancy."

Mallory nodded. "I agree. And there may be more elsewhere. But for now let's take a look at the files." He turned to Fielding. "OK to walk across the floor?"

"Go ahead. It's been checked."

Mallory moved over to the desk, lifted the top file off the pile and placed it on its own to one side. Then he carefully pulled back the cover, revealing a single sheet of paper inside. It was a Xerox copy of an original document, and had a health centre logo at the top.

Mallory scanned the document, then looked through another half dozen or so of the files. Then he called to Falcon who had stayed by the door.

"We're in the right place. Carol Devril's been here, and at least we know now how she got hold of the data on the babies she abducted. The papers in the files are copies of health centre documents."

He put the files back into a stack, and told the technicians they could bag them as evidence. Then he joined the others at the door and they continued the tour.

The cloister ran around the four sides of the building and enclosed a rectangle of ground that looked as if it had once been a garden. Now, illuminated by a searchlight, it was a tangled mass of brambles and dead grass with a stone-rimmed well in the centre.

"We're checking the well later when a underwater unit arrive. But on that side." Fielding pointed to a small area behind a plastic windbreak. "There are signs that the ground's been dug up. We're carrying out a search now, but it's a painstaking job and it may be some time before we know if anything's buried there."

"We'll look around the rest of the place." Mallory had to contain his impatience, but he knew the importance of collecting every scrap of available evidence *in situ*.

They left the cloisters at the end opposite the entrance hall and went into the hospital proper. Here, there were two long narrow wards, with a number of smaller rooms off them. Beyond the wards there was a small operating theatre complex.

Fielding led the way into the operating theatre. There was a faint smell of chloroform hanging heavy on the air, and in the emergency lighting Hannah thought the scene was like a time capsule. An illustration out of a medical history book.

The arched roof and the walls had once been painted white, but large areas were now disfigured by green mould. One wall was tiled to a height of about six feet and three porcelain sinks, almost as large as baths, stood against it on legs. Benches with drawers underneath covered the lower portions of the other three walls. Above the benches a single shelf ran around the room. There were glass bottles of various sizes on the shelf, some thickly ridged and dark brown in colour. Glass-fronted metal cabinets and metal trolleys were scattered around the floor, their rusting surfaces covered with syringes, stethoscopes and a variety of enamel bowls, some small and kidney-shaped others large with handles. And on one trolley, surgical instruments were arranged in neat rows; scalpels of all sizes, drills, and saws, all rusted now with age.

The operating table, which was adjustable in height and tilt, stood in the centre of the floor under a battery of ceiling lights. Around the table there was an array of trolleys, metal bins and anaesthetic equipment. But some things were glaringly out of place in that time capsule; the top of the operating table, and one of the trolleys, had been covered in fresh white paper towelling. Two kidney-shaped bowls were standing on the trolley, and by the side of them there were two rows of neatly arranged implements. One was a selection of shiny new scalpels, and the other a line of metal meat skewers.

As soon as the inspection was complete, a scene-of-crime officer started to bag various items to be taken away for further analysis.

"Just one more site." Fielding led the way out of the operating theatre, along a short corridor, and into a small box-like room. A row of wooden cupboards ran along one wall and Fielding opened one of them.

"Towels, uniforms, caps and masks. The full works. It seems nobody bothered to clean them out when the place was abandoned."

"So we know where the nurse's uniform came from, and . . ."

Mallory was interrupted a by a shout which echoed along the corridor from the direction of the cloisters. The party moved back quickly, and as they crossed the wards and came out into the open air Falcon was ahead. He moved across the flags to the edge of the cloister and leaned over the plastic windbreak. Inside, one of the technicians was pointing downwards.

Falcon stopped and cursed. A litany of blasphemies. Bones, partly covered with decaying flesh lay exposed against the black soil. The remains of a child's body.

It was out of a nightmare. A vision that had no place in the world that Falcon knew, and he felt that he was looking at something out of a nightmare. It was the eyes that held his gaze. Or rather, the sockets where the eyes should have been. Just dark holes now with metal skewers sticking out of them.

In the next few minutes the team of technicians carefully brushed away the soil from a line of skeletons. But only one more had skewers where the eyes had been. The others had their arms neatly folded and looked as if they'd simply fallen asleep.

"This is not . . ." Falcon groped for the words. "Not human. Whoever did this is outside the pale."

"Right." Mallory forced himself to concentrate. To ignore the final disappointment. All hope that the children were still alive had been shattered by the sight of that mass grave. When he spoke, it was in short, sharp sentences, as if his mind could no longer cope with anything complicated.

"I'm going to report to the chief constable — in person. Explain what we've found here. You call the FME and tell him we need a full path team here urgently. When they arrive, let them take over. But you stay on site to coordinate events as they happen. I'll get back to talk to the medics as soon as I can. Oh, and apparently the front door had to be forced. So try to find out how Carol Devril got into the building. Hannah are you—"

He stopped suddenly as he looked at Hannah. Her eyes were fixed on point on the other side of the cloisters, and her mind was obviously somewhere else.

"Hannah?"

"Oh, sorry, I was miles away. Did you want something?"

"I was explaining that I was going to report to the chief constable. Do you want to stay here until I get back?"

She shook her head. "No, I'm going back to the flat. It's late, but I want to access the data on my computer. Something's happened here that I don't understand, and I want to go through all the data on the case. Try to find what I've missed."

Mallory thought she seemed disturbed. And for some reason he wondered if was just because of what she'd just seen in that terrible grave.

Or was there something else?

CHAPTER 27

Mallory was right. Something was bothering her.

Nagging away at the back of her mind as she sat by the window looking out into the darkness. It was there, on the far edge of her thoughts, but she couldn't place it. Then it came to her.

The house.

Hannah realised then that it was something about the house that was bothering her. What were the words in the scene-of-crime report: *Apart from the fact that it was half burnt-out, it appeared to be a normal family home.*

'A normal family home.'

That was it. That was what was nagging away at the back of her mind. Was it possible that there was nothing at all in the house that spoke of Carol Devril's other life? A life that was most certainly not normal.

Yes, it was possible, Hannah had to concede that. Because Carol Devril must have appeared to be leading just such a normal life. Or, at least, she wouldn't have presented as a serial killer. But what if something *had* been left behind at the house. Something that both the fire investigators and the scene-of-crime unit had missed because they'd not been looking for it.

Or perhaps it was something else. Something she was almost afraid to think about. An echo trapped in the bricks and mortar.

She remembered something Father David had once said when she'd asked him if it was possible to leave a trace behind in a place where evil had been committed. At the time, they'd been investigating the case of a man accused of murdering his wife in a gruesome ritual killing. Hannah and Father David had visited the place where the man had carried out the murder. It was in a derelict out building at an isolated cottage in East Anglia and as soon as they were inside Hannah had sensed something in the air. The experience had frightened her, and it was then she'd asked the question, and she'd never forgotten Father David's chilling reply.

"Oh, yes. There are many well-documented instances of a trace being left where evil has occurred. But usually it is only a certain kind of person who is able to pick up the signals. And it would seem that you are one of those people."

She knew that she had to visit the Devril house, and taste the atmosphere of the place where the small boy had died. But the idea filled her with dread. Not because of what she might find trapped in the ruins of the place. That didn't bother her. What terrified her was that she might again be able to sense something that was lurking there under the surface.

She looked at watch, and saw it was almost half past one. For a moment she almost decided it was too late to go that day. But she knew it was too important to leave and she called the Operations Centre. The duty officer told her that Chief Superintendent Mallory was still with the chief constable, but when she explained what she wanted he agreed to allocate a police car and two officers to take her to the Devril house.

* * *

The crescent of abandoned houses was in deep shadow with none of the ornate street lights working. In the darkness the bare branches of the plane trees seemed to enclose the place like the bars of a cage.

The house was boarded up, but as one of the police officers held a torch on the door the other used a claw hammer to pull away the planks nailed across the frame. The two officers were reluctant to let her enter the house alone, and in the end she had to agree to let them wait inside by the front door.

They'd given her a powerful torch and she shone it ahead as she entered the lobby. The first thing that struck her was the smell. Musty, airless, and still carrying a strong tinge of charred wood. She remembered what Mallory had told her about a petrol bomb being thrown through a glass panel in the front door. It was clear that the short narrow lobby had borne the brunt of the blaze and as she moved forward she had to step carefully over the spaces where the floorboards had gone, exposing the skeleton of the supporting beams underneath. There were two doors off the side of the lobby and one at the far end by the remains of the stairs.

Hannah opened the door on the left and looked inside. And she was surprised. Apart from a series of deep scorch marks around the door frame, and a layer of thick soot on every surface, the room looked undisturbed. She moved the torch around, examining the interior. In the centre there was a large pine table with four chairs arranged around it, and a dresser with crockery on the shelves against one wall. It was obviously the dining room and didn't appear to have been used for anything else.

The door on the right was leaning on its hinges and she had to twist it to force it open. This room must have been nearer to the source of the fire and had suffered more damage than the dining room. Bu it wasn't completely gutted, and the light from the torch revealed a strangely colourless scene frozen in shades of black and grey. The wallpaper, once heavily patterned, hung in strips from the plaster, the ends curled and shrivelled. Hannah jumped suddenly as she swung the torch around and caught a dull flash of light. She brought the beam back and looked again. The flash had come from a mirror over the fireplace, the surface dulled with tendrils of smoke.

This must have been the living room and it was full of the memories of a family's life. Photographs and the remains of charred magazines were scattered around on shelves and the mantelpiece, all covered in a thick coat of black smog particles, and there was even a bowl of fruit, reduced now to a mass of wrinkled skins, on a chest of drawers. But the most poignant reminder of what the room had once been was the abandoned game of Monopoly on a table by the window, the dice and counters still out on the blackened board and piles of what had once been play money arranged in front of the two chairs.

As she looked around, Hannah formed a mental picture of Jason playing the game with the babysitter. According to David Mallory, the two of them had died on the landing, so maybe Jason had had to go to bed before the game ended. But then they must have left the bedroom after the noise of the explosion, only to be trapped on the landing with the stairs gone. Trapped there to die inhaling the deadly mixture of smoke and chemical fumes from the solvents left in the hall. The thought filled her with a great sadness that so young a life had ended there. But despite that feeling of deep melancholy, she was strangely disappointed. She had expected more. To feel something hanging in the air of that museum of trapped memories. Perhaps she'd been wrong to come here, she thought.

She sighed, a long drawn-out sound and moved back into the lobby. Ahead of her the stairs had gone, collapsed onto the floor below. All that was left now was the remains of a few charred banister rails hanging precariously over a drop. She shone the torch through the tangle of wood piled on the floor and made out the shape of a small door in the far wall. Carefully she moved through the wreckage and lifted the latch on the wooden panel. Inside, the torchlight revealed a flight of steps leading onto a stone flagged floor.

She shone the torch around and realised she was looking at Peter Devril's work room. A carpenter's wooden bench with built-in vice ran along the length of one wall, and there was a rack of tools above it. In a corner various sized lengths of timber were neatly arranged against the side of a tall metal cupboard.

Nothing out of the ordinary. And yet she hesitated as she stood at the top of the stairs. Then she shrugged and started down. The cellar had escaped most of the fire damage and at first she simply walked around, shinning the torch onto the brick walls and the long bench. Then she moved in front of the metal cupboard. The double doors had been forced, probably by the scene-of-crime unit, and they opened easily. The space inside was divided into two sections. On the left, a stack of shelves was filled with tins of paint, jars of nails and brushes, all arranged in neat rows. A rail, with a number of large clips attached to it, ran across the top of the right-hand side, but nothing was hanging there now and she remembered Peter Devril's brother had said the clowns used to be kept in a locked steel cupboard. But they'd gone now.

She closed the door and was turning away when she heard the noise in the darkness. She whirled round, panic-stricken, the beam of the torch swinging wildly across the floor. Then the light touched something in the corner opposite the metal cupboard. Two points of red brightness reflected back in the darkness. She brought the torch back and for a moment the shape was caught there, frozen in the beam of light — a large sleek rat with a long curved tail. Hannah stifled a scream as it stood there, seemingly mesmerised by the light. Then it was gone.

She shone the light on the wall behind the spot where the creature had been crouching. There was an archway in the brick, leading into another space. She crossed the floor and shone the torch inside, mindful of the rat that had run there. She saw it again, against the far wall, then it disappeared through a gap in the bricks, and she felt a surge of relief when she realised it had an escape route.

She stepped into room and shone the torch round again. The walls were covered in peeling whitewash and there was a long slate covered bench along one side of the room, with a number of metal hooks driven into the wall above it. They were presumably for hanging game, and Hannah guessed the place had originally been some kind of pantry.

As she continued to sweep the light round she saw a wooden panel fixed to the far wall over a small square sink. She crossed the floor and looked more closely at the panel. Rows of nails had been driven into the surface for utensils to hang on, but they were all rusty now in the rotted wood.

She felt it then.

For the first time since she'd entered the house she felt a sense of foreboding. As she stood there looking at the wooden panel, the air seemed to become thick and heavy. The same thing had happened in East Anglia and now, as then, it carried with it a sense that evil was lurking in the bricks and mortar. Trapped in the fabric of the building.

She leaned forward and examined the wooden panel. At first, it appeared to be attached to the wall by several rusted screws, but when she touched the edge she felt a slight movement. She placed the torch in the sink, with the beam directed at the wall, and moved her hands over the panel. There seemed to be more movement towards the top and when she held onto two of the nails and lifted, the panel came away. Behind, there was a recess in the wall between two stone lintels.

When she saw what was there she caught her breath.

The wall at the back of the recess was covered with a sheet of red velvet, with a border of golden tassels hanging from the top. At the base the lower lintel formed a shelf, and there was a tall brass candlestick at either end. A silver-coloured photo frame stood next to each of the candlesticks, with another in the centre of the shelf. A small ornately engraved metal box stood in front of each photo frame.

Hannah picked up the torch to look more closely, then leaned forward and with her free hand lifted the photo frame next to the right-hand candlestick. The photograph, which was in colour and looked as if it had been taken with instant camera, was of a young girl strapped to what looked like a trolley. Her eyes were wide open, with an expression of fear more intense than Hannah had ever seen. Hannah put the photograph back and picked up the metal box. There was a clasp in front and when she flicked it with thumb the top opened. Inside, resting on a patch of white silk, there was a lock of hair. The picture in front of the left hand candlestick was also of a young child, a boy this time, and it appeared to have been taken in the same place with the body strapped to a trolley. But now the child's eyes were closed. When Hannah looked in the metal box in front of the photo frame she found it contained another lock of hair.

What she was looking at was a shrine. A temple hidden away from prying eyes. It only seemed to be dedicated to the abductions carried out after the family had moved into the house, and there was no record of any earlier crimes. Perhaps they were celebrated elsewhere, Hannah thought.

The shrine was a typical artefact in the classic behaviour pattern of the serial killer. A place to display the trophies of their crimes. A private place where the killer could come and experience again the sense of power, the knowledge that they were in ultimate control. And finally sense the feeling of release that the crimes had brought. That rush of ego-sustaining adrenaline that had become so necessary to their twisted lives.

But something was wrong here.

Hannah guessed the locks of hair in the boxes were from the first two abductions and that Carol Devril had kept them as trophies. But why had the pattern changed after the first two killings? And come to that, where were the photographs of the other victims?

Hannah moved the light onto the third frame in the centre of the shelf. This was no toddler. This was the school photograph of a boy who looked to be around six or seven. The Toybreaker had selected an older child as her next victim. Hannah flicked open the box in front of the photograph. It was empty. Clearly, Carol Devril had not killed the child yet. Which meant that she must have had that photograph *before* taking the victim. And when Hannah looked closely at the photograph, she knew why. Because she recognised the boy from the photograph taken after the fire.

It was Jason.

At that moment Hannah realised the truth, and all her perceptions fell apart. The Toybreaker had fooled them. This case wasn't about Carol Devril changing personality as a result of Jason's death in the fire. It never had been.

And she had to warn Falcon before it was too late.

CHAPTER 28

Falcon had arranged for the pathology team to be brought to the site, and he was standing in the shelter of the cloisters when a uniformed officer approached and told him that a Father Michael wanted to see Chief Superintendent Mallory. Falcon told him to bring the priest through the cordon and walked to the main door to meet him.

When the priest arrived, Falcon explained that Mallory had left but would be back later that evening. Father Michael was carrying an old leather briefcase and he opened it and took out a folded sheet of paper which he passed to Falcon.

"I thought this might be useful for your search. It's a plan of the original building that I got from the diocesan records, but it took longer to locate than I expected."

Falcon opened out the sheet. There were three architectural plans drawn on the paper, and that puzzled him. Until he suddenly realised what he was looking at.

"This building has a cellar." It wasn't a question.

"A crypt, yes. And it has a somewhat chequered history. The asylum was built on the site of a much older building. A dispensary, I think, that was originally run by monks, and during that time the laboratory to prepare medicines was in the crypt."

"So where was the access to the crypt?" Mallory asked.

"When the monks used it, the entrance was via a flight of steps leading down from the cloisters. But the steps were sealed off during the reign of Queen Elizabeth I. At that time the Faith was under attack and part of the crypt was converted to a secret chapel and living quarters for a priest."

"But if the steps were sealed there must have been some other way of getting into the crypt."

"Too be sure there was. A way in from up here and an escape to the outside via a tunnel. But no one's ever been able to find the tunnel."

"What about the way in from this side."

"No problem. There's a flight of steps hidden behind a statue in what's now the entrance hall."

"Can you take me into the crypt and guide me around?"

"Yes, I can do that."

"Right, I'll get the armed response unit to provide cover. Then we can see what's down there."

Inside the hall, Falcon followed Father Michael across the floor towards the far side where the marble staircase swept upwards. At regular intervals stone statues were set at floor level in niches in the walls. Father Michael stopped in front of one of them. In the niche behind it there was a narrow arch, and the priest backed into it. When he was in position he bent down and lifted a rectangular stone which was set into the floor, and placed it against the wall. Both Falcon and Father Michael had been supplied with powerful torches and as Falcon shone the beam of his torch downwards it revealed a flight of steps where the stone had been removed. Two members of the armed response unit went down first, but Falcon had told them to wait at the bottom of the steps. He needed to have support in the crypt, but he didn't want anyone just blundering in.

The steps led down onto the flagged floor of a low passage. The two armed officers stayed back, one on either side of the passage, and another member of the unit rigged up a mobile spotlight. It might be needed later, but Falcon wanted to move in with as much surprise as he could, and he'd told the officer to keep the light switched off for the time being. Everything was in darkness as Falcon and Father Michael moved forward, and for a moment Falcon thought he saw a dim light ahead. But after a few yards, the passage appeared to open up and Falcon was forced to turn his torch on to get his bearings. They were in a vaulted room and Falcon saw the priest cross himself.

"The old chapel." Father Michael put his mouth close to Falcon's ear and whispered the words, his voice low and differential.

The walls and floor of the chapel were plain stone, and simple wooden chairs had been set in front of a table that had obviously served as an altar. On it, Falcon could see two candle sticks gleaming in the light.

Then suddenly a figure seemed to materialise out of the gloom, emerging from a passage at the right of the altar. It was wearing a white uniform and a face mask, and beckoned to them.

"Our Father . . ." The priest began to intone a prayer, but Falcon ignored him. This was no ghost, he was sure of that and he started to move towards it.

"Carol Devril," Falcon kept his voice quiet. "I'm arresting you for the . . ."

But she suddenly twisted around and disappeared behind the altar. Falcon ran forward and he saw that she'd entered a small space directly behind the altar. The end was blocked by a wall and the only way out was through a tiny arch set into the stonework.

Carol Devril reached the arch but realising that Falcon was too close behind, she whipped round to face him. He was still holding the torch and too late he realised that Carol Devril was grasping a length of metal pipe in her hand. Falcon's arm stretched forward and the fingers of his free hand connected with the fabric of the mask, dragging it sideways and revealing the face of the figure in the light from the torch.

For no more than a second, Falcon gazed on the features of that face. But it was enough.

"No!" he screamed out the single word as the pipe smashed down on the side of his head. As he fell, his mobile rang.

* * *

"So what happened at the asylum?" Hannah asked.

She was back with Mallory in the chief superintendent's office at the Operations Centre.

"I'm not entirely sure yet. But I think I can piece most of it together from what Father Michael told me. Apparently, there's a crypt below the old asylum and Falcon and Father Michael went down there with back-up from officers of the armed response unit. There's a chapel in the crypt and Carol Devril was there. She was wearing the nurse's uniform, and she ran off when she realised they were coming after her. Falcon gave chase, but she clobbered him with an iron pipe and escaped through a passage behind the altar. Apparently, the passage was some kind of escape tunnel from the days when the chapel was used for secret worship, and it could be sealed off with a stone which she knocked into place. Anyway, by the time the armed response officers freed it, Carol Devril was long gone."

"And Father Michael saw her."

"Oh, yes. She was wearing the uniform and mask. It seems that Falcon pulled the mask away just before he was hit, and he screamed out then. Presumably because he saw the burns on her face."

"How's Falcon now?"

"He's not come round yet, but they've done all the tests in A & E, and they don't think it's that serious. According to one of the nurses, he's got a skull like granite and . . ."

He was interrupted as one of the phones on his desk rang. He picked up the receiver and listened. When he put it down again there was a strange expression on his face.

"Falcon didn't scream because of the state of Carol Devil's face. He couldn't have done."

"Why not?"

"That was a report from the asylum. Scene-of-crime unit have found a body in the well. It seems it's that of Carol Devril. And she's been dead for some months." He scratched the fingers of one hand across his jaw. "So who the hell hit Falcon?"

Hannah didn't answer. Instead she asked a question of her own. "Can they be certain the body is that of Carol Devril?"

"Proof?" Mallory shook his head. "Not yet. But from what they just told me I'm certain in my own mind."

"Why?" Hannah pressed home the point, wanting to be absolutely sure before she committed herself.

"One, the body is that of a woman. Two, the age is about right. Three, the well is close to the children's burial ground. And four, she had metal skewers driven into her eyes. Oh, it's all circumstantial at the moment, I grant you. But I'm certain, all right. It's Carol Devril's body. So, I repeat the question. Who clobbered Falcon? Because whoever it was, was dressed in the nurse's uniform."

Hannah decided it was time to drop the bombshell. It was just a pity it was too late.

"We've all been wrong, David. From the beginning. You see, the Toybreaker wasn't just one person. It was two different people. One just took over from the other. And that's what we didn't see."

Mallory looked at her closely. "So who hit Falcon?"

"The person who carried out the last four abductions."

"And who was that?"

"Oh, that was Peter Devril."

CHAPTER 29

"It was just a pity I didn't get to Falcon earlier. It I had, I could have warned him about Peter Devril."

Mallory shook his head. "Christ, there's no way any of us could have foreseen this." He was still trying to come to terms with what she'd told him. "But you're sure about it? Absolutely sure, I mean?"

"I am now. There were two killers."

"Two of them?" Mallory sounded weary beyond words.

"Yes. The mistake we made from the beginning was that none of us realised the most important change in the MO was the fact that the locks of hair were only left behind *after* the first two abductions. We looked for a common thread running through all the crimes, and we found one. The clowns that were left behind at the crime scenes. It was the perfect link because we knew all the clowns came from the same source. And that's what fooled us all along. We were trying to fit an evolving behaviour profile to a single killer, while in fact the Toybreaker was two people. We were right about Carol Devril, but she was only one of the killers."

"And the other was Peter Devril." Mallory suddenly snapped his fingers. "That must have been why Falcon yelled out when he ripped the mask off. He was expecting to see the face of Carol Devril. Instead he was confronted by Peter Devril."

"So how did Devril get in and out of the asylum?"

"The passage at the rear of the chapel in the crypt led out into a thicket of scrubs on the other side of the wall that encloses the old people's home. According to Father Michael it must be the escape route that was used by the priests in the past. The thicket was the place where Peter Devril used to play with Jason, and he obviously found the passage and used it to get in and out of the asylum. That was how he gave the officers the slip earlier. And he must have been inside the building when the search started."

Mallory ran a hand across his eyes, and Hannah thought he looked as if he'd aged ten years in the past few days. "I've got a meeting with the press office people in ten minutes. They want to fine tune the statement they're going to put out at a news conference in the morning. Their priority is to contain the situation the best way they can."

"Not easy," Hannah said. "Not with the city still on the edge."

"You're right, but the woman in charge, Cathleen Forster, is an ex-reporter with a lot of experience in newspapers and radio. She's smart, and she's already mapping out a strategy."

"So what does she plan to tell the media?"

"She's already roughed out a preliminary statement saying that we've found a body we believe to be that of Carol Devril. So now we're concentrating the search on her husband, Peter Devril, who we still think can help us with our inquiries. God knows, it's thin enough, but by making it a formal statement we can avoid direct questions at this stage. We'll also give out the location where Carol

Devril's body was found, because it will be impossible to keep it secret with all the police presence still in the area."

"And what about finding the bodies of the children? Will you go public with that?"

"Absolutely not. The priority there has to be the mothers. The identification of the bodies is going to be difficult and harrowing for them, and until the family liaison unit is completely satisfied that they've done all they can, we keep the fact that we've found the remains under wraps. Give the families time to grieve in private. God knows, it's not much, but at least it's something we can do for them."

He was quiet for a moment, thinking. When he spoke again it was as if he had to force the words out.

"What made Peter Devril do things that were that evil? And to little children."

"I don't understand all the factors yet, but some of them are becoming clearer. Peter Devril was what people used to call not all there. But he only began to develop a damaged personality after he'd met his wife. She was a control freak and she distorted his mind, to the extent that he reacted to certain trigger events."

"Do we know what these events are now?"

"I think the first was when he came across a shrine at the cellar of the house. I haven't had chance to fill you in yet, but it was something I found there."

She told him then about her visit to the house.

"And this was a shrine?" Mallory sounded puzzled.

"Yes. Or a trophy cabinet, if you like."

"So she kept it to remind her about the crimes she'd committed?"

"Well, it's not quite that simple. A reminder, yes. But it's my guess that the shrine was also a place where she could once again experience the power she'd possessed when she'd carried out the murders, and then feel the release the killings must have brought."

"So how does the shrine fit into the picture as far as Peter Devril is concerned?"

"Everything depends on the time sequence. The SOCO found a body that we can be sure is that of Carol Devril. And because of the location of the body, and the skewers in the eyes, we can also be sure that Peter Devril killed her."

"Agreed."

"We also know that Peter Devril took over the role of the Toybreaker. It must have been after Carol Devril was dead, and on the basis of the changes in MO we can assume that she was killed sometime between the second and third abductions."

"But why did he kill her?"

"That's where the shrine comes into the picture. Peter Devril must have found it."

"How can you know that?"

"The eyes at the jar in the museum came from the shrine. And they must have been put there by Peter Devril because if our time sequence based on changes in the Toybreaker's MO is right, Carol Devril was already dead. So we can establish for certain that Peter Devril knew about the shrine. And that was why he killed Carol."

"Because of the shrine?"

"Because of what he found in it. A photograph of her next victim. Jason."

"Jesus. She would have killed her own child?"

"It happens."

"But wait a minute," Mallory sounded confused. "If Peter Devril knew Jason was to be the next victim, why didn't he just take the boy and run? Hide away with him and start a new life somewhere?"

"But he couldn't, could he? Because Carol Devril had already told him that if he stepped out of line she'd tell the police that he was the Toybreaker, and he knew they'd never stop looking for him then. No, she'd boxed him into a corner, and in his mental state there was only one sure way he could protect Jason from her. By taking her life."

"But Jason . . ." Mallory's voice trailed away.

"Jason died in the fire," Hannah finished the sentence for him. "The second trigger event. The ultimate irony. Peter Devril kills his wife to protect Jason. Then the boy dies on him."

"It must have torn him apart, I can understand that. What I don't understand is why he took on the role of the Toybreaker?" Mallory was still struggling to come to terms with everything he'd learned.

"That's the crux of the whole thing. Everything revolves around the trigger events, which both involved major traumas. In the first, he killed his wife, and in the second Jason died in the fire. God knows, they'd be difficult enough for anybody to cope with. But in Peter Devril's fragmented state it's no wonder they tipped him over the edge, and made a normally caring person crave revenge. In his mind, someone had to suffer for Jason's death. So Peter Devril picked on other children. And he had a readymade set-up. Everything was in place and he simply took over the mantle of the Toybreaker."

"How did Carol Devril know about the old asylum?."

"We have to guess here, but I think Peter Devril and the boy stumbled on the secret entrance to the building when they were playing in that thicket, and they must have told Carol about it. And in turn, she must have thought the asylum was a perfect base for her activities."

"It's all starting to fall into place now." Mallory ran a hand across his eyes. "All the loose ends. For one thing, we can guess now why Peter Devril claimed his wife died in the fire. So no one would find out that he'd killed her himself."

"Makes sense," Hannah agreed.

"And one more loose end. We know now why there'd been no sightings of Carol Devril over the past few months. Falcon was wrong there. Even in this day and age of electronic data gathering there's still one place to hide.

"The grave," Hannah whispered the words.

"Yes, the grave."

CHAPTER 30

"Something's still bothering you isn't it?" Hannah sensed that Mallory was troubled.

"Yes, it is. I can't get my head round the fact that Peter Devril changed personalities completely and became a child killer. Just like that."

"Oh, I very much doubt it was *just like that.* We saw evidence of the struggle inside him in the way he handled the locks of hair at the crime scenes. But I think that in the end, his mind had been so messed-up by Carol Devril that the evil personality took over."

"How did it do that?"

"These things are never simple, and I don't understand the mechanics of it yet. But we can be sure that the evil did take over, even to the point where Peter Devril sent the message we found at the museum. A message telling us he didn't care any longer. That was part of the battle."

"But he was still able to talk to us rationally when we interviewed him. He didn't let any of this show."

"He'd become very cunning by that time. Which is not unusual with this kind of personality."

"So Carol Devril's to blame for everything." It wasn't a question.

"In a sense, yes. I haven't got all the pieces yet, but from what I can put together, I think I can get the general picture."

"Go on."

"Carol was a serial killer before she met Peter Devril. A serial killer who murdered little children. But she did it in secret, and that was obviously enough to satisfy her at the time. Then she met a man she could completely control and she married him. Maybe that filled a gap in her life and she no longer felt the compulsion to kill. But then Jason was born and she found the control she had over Peter Devril was getting weaker. And that must have made her angry. Angry enough to start killing again. But this time her demons demanded more. Taking the lives of little children, and making it look like natural causes, was no longer enough. She was angry at her husband for turning away from her, and she was angry at her son because he was the cause of it. That was why she used the clowns. Peter Devril had made them for Jason and to her they were a symbol of the way she'd been shut out by the two of them. The smashed clown was left behind as a defiant message. To hell with both her husband and her son."

"So the clowns were symbolic. When she was smashing them, she was destroying her husband and son?"

For the first time that evening Hannah found herself smiling. "Why, Chief Superintendent, if I didn't know any better, I'd say you were beginning to see something in all this psychological mumbo-jumbo."

"Point taken." Mallory almost smiled himself. "But what about the locks of hair? What part did they play in all this?"

"For Carol Devril they were simply souvenirs for her trophy cabinet. But for Peter Devril they were something for the mothers to remember their children by. And that was the big giveaway. The change in MO after the second abduction. Carol Devril took the hair away, Peter Devril left it behind. But we all missed the real significance of that."

"We missed too many things. Right from the start. This whole case has been a sod."

"True, but now we have to try and move forward." Hannah was determined to lift his mood.

"You're right, of course. Time enough for inquests later. But there's one aspect of the case still puzzling me. Peter Devril wanted revenge, and I can go along with that. It's the other stuff I'm having difficulty with. Like the mask and the meat skewers."

"He wore the mask when he carried out the abductions so that no one would recognise him. And he wore the nurse's uniform to make people think he was a woman. But the skewers were different. We know now from what was found at the mass grave that Peter Devril didn't use the skewers when he killed the children. I don't think he would ever have been capable of that. But he knew the skewers had been part of the ritual when Carol murdered the little ones. So he must have thought it was fitting to use them on her when he killed her."

"He must really have hated her."

"Not surprising really, when you think that she'd been about to kill Jason. Carol Devril was an evil, evil killer praying on a vulnerable man."

"I see," Mallory said, although he wasn't sure he did. "Look, all I want now is nail the bastard."

"We have to bring him in, I agree. The more his personality became fragmented the more he began to lose control, and by now there may be very little of the real Peter Devril left."

"So he will carry on killing little children?"

"Oh, yes. The lust for revenge is in total control now, and there's no doubt he'll kill again. No doubt at all."

CHAPTER 31

As Mallory sat by the fire, one single thought dominated his mind. Peter Devril was the Toybreaker, and they'd let him go.

There was no shirking it. If Devril killed again he, David Mallory, would be responsible for the deaths of more children. And even after having his emotions blunted by years in the service, he wasn't sure he could live with that. Not this time. Not after what he'd seen at the old asylum.

There was only one way out of the dilemma. One way to stop the torment that was starting to tear at his mind. And that was to catch Peter Devril before he killed again. But for that Mallory needed time, and with Clayborn baying for his blood that might be the one thing he didn't have.

The doorbell rang and Mallory let the man in.

"It was too late for the pubs, and it's good of you to come out here." Mallory pulled another chair closer to the fire, "But some things are best not said over the phone."

"Like what happened tonight at the old asylum?"

"You know about that already?" Mallory wasn't really surprised.

"I got a call from the chief constable earlier. He put me in the picture and we arranged a meeting of the Senior Management Group for a full briefing at eight tomorrow morning. You'll be asked to attend, of course."

"So they can give me my marching orders?"

"David, I won't pretend that you're flavour of the month at the moment. Too many problems with this investigation. But let's not lose sight of the overriding success. From what you told me on the phone, you've identified this man Peter Devril as the Toybreaker. True, the media might not see it as such a success, particularly as you had him in your hands at one time, but the officers on the Senior Management Group will recognise it as the excellent piece of detection it was."

"Thanks, but I'm not sure all of them will take that view."

"Ah, you mean friend Clayborn."

"Yes."

"A word to the wise, David. If I were you, I wouldn't worry too much about him just at the moment."

"Why not? I had the Toybreaker and I let him go. You know as well as I do that Clayborn will put the knife in and demand I'm taken off the investigation. Maybe even go for a charge of professional incompetence."

"Oh I agree, that's exactly what he would do."

"So why don't I have to worry about him then?"

"Let's just say that right now Clayborn has problems of his own, and that he won't be at tomorrow's meeting of the Senior Management Group." He was quiet for a moment. "No, I don't believe that you'll be taken off the investigation. Not just now, anyway. So find this Peter Devril before he kills again. You'll be a bloody hero then, Chief Superintendent. A bloody hero. Now get your single malt out."

CHAPTER 32

Because of Mallory's commitments the next day's briefing had been put back to half past one in the afternoon. But even then he was late and when Hannah arrived at the Operations Centre she was surprised to see Falcon in the chief superintendent's office. He had a bandage around his forehead, but he looked well enough.

"Shouldn't you still be in hospital?" Hannah asked as he raised a hand in greeting.

"That's what the doctor said," Falcon agreed. "But I persuaded him to let me go."

"Walked out on him, more likely," Falcon didn't contradict her. "Where's the Chief Super?"

"He had to attend a meeting of the Senior Management Group and it went on longer than expected."

"They crucified him?"

"No, oddly enough they didn't. He's still on the case, and right now he's with the press officer. But he asked me to bring you up to speed. First, though, congratulations on figuring out the Toybreaker scenario."

"Thanks, but I should have seen it earlier."

"What, the fact that there were two killers? Come on, I don't think I'd have come up with that however long I'd been on the case." He waved her to a seat and sat down himself. "So, a situation report. We've upgraded the search for Peter Devril. All the stops out."

"I think he's holed up somewhere around here?"

"Why?"

"This is his back yard, and he's got unfinished business here. I already told David that Peter Devril won't stop now."

"She did." Mallory came into the office and closed the door behind him. To Hannah he seemed less stressed than the last time she'd seen him.

"So we have to find Devril because he'll kill again. Problem is, we don't know where to look. The Devril house, the old asylum and his hide away down by the docks are all under surveillance, of course, but we don't think he'll go back to any of those. So all we can do is rely on the public. We'd already had sightings of him from the first time we ran the search. We put them to one side once we had him in custody, but we're checking them out and integrating them with the new sightings. And we're plotting all the data to see if we can establish a 'movement/time' pattern. But we haven't been able to tap the best potential source yet."

"And who's that?" Hannah asked.

"John Devril. He might be able to suggest somewhere his brother's gone to ground, but there's no one at his address just now."

"So while we've got a spare moment, what about the tape we found at the asylum?" Hannah asked.

"You're in luck there. Forensics made the copy you asked for and sent it round this morning. I haven't had time to listen to it yet, so we can play it now if you like."

There was a tape recorder on the desk and he took a cassette from a drawer, placed in the machine and pressed the playback button. A long hiss of static came through the speakers, followed by the sound of giggling. Then more static as there was an attempt to control the giggling.

Finally, a sweet young voice began to sing. Hesitantly at first, then slowly gaining in confidence.

"Away in a manger, no crib for a bed."

When the carol was finished an adult voice cut in.

"Now glue the manger together, the one you coloured and cut out of the card. That's it. And put Mary and Joseph in. Then the animals. Now, what's left?"

"Baby Jesus."

"That's right. Baby Jesus. Now, what about another carol? What else did you learn at school?"

"I know." There was a pause, then the sweet voice again.

"Once in Royal David's city, stood a lowly cattle shed."

When it was finished the adult voice cut in again.

"That was very good. And what do we do now, do you know?"

"Yes."

It was a shout. *"The presents."*

"That's right, the presents. Do you remember what I said? The presents are just for the two of us. Just you and me. You mustn't say anything to Mummy about them, must you?

"No, it's just you and me. But doesn't Mummy like Christmas anymore? She used to like it. We used to have a good time at Christmas."

"I know we did."

"So why can't we all have a Christmas this year?"

"Things might get better. Next year perhaps." There was a great sadness in the voice now.

"It's all right." Now it was the young voice struggling to be reassuring. *"We've still got the presents round the tree. Look what I've got for you."*

"For me?" There was the sound of paper being torn. *"Oh, thank you, Jason."*

"Is it what you wanted? I saved up for ages for it."

"A box of paints. It's exactly what I wanted."

At that point a loud burst of static cut in. It was obviously a technical fault and the recording finished there.

For a moment no one spoke, then Hannah broke the silence. "Things must have been getting bad at home. So bad that Peter Devril and his son had to stage their own private Christmas. Carols, presents and even a tree, by the sound of it."

"But why would he have wanted to record it?" Mallory asked.

"Times remembered." It was Falcon who answered, thinking of his own kids. "For parents there are always defining moments in the life of a child that are very special. Moments that stay trapped in time. When they take their first step, when they draw their first picture and hand it to you, when they go to school for the first time. Those moments become more precious as a child grows up, and parents like to hold onto them. To keep them alive in their memory."

Hannah looked at him and smiled, touched by the glimpse of another layer of the chief inspector's personality. "You're right. I think that was what Peter Devril was doing. He wanted the tape to capture things the way they were. But the difference here was that there were only certain moments he could capture. Moments that only the two them, him and Jason, could share because they had to be kept secret from the boy's mother. I think that tape's one of the saddest things I've ever heard. Can I take it away, please? I'd like to study it in more detail later."

Mallory took the tape out of the machine and handed it to Hannah who slipped it into her handbag.

"So why did Peter Devril keep the tape at the asylum?" Falcon asked.

"Like you said, times remembered," Hannah's voice was soft. "How it used to be when the boy was alive. When they were happy together. Just the two of them."

She turned away, fighting to hold back the tears. Not wanting to show an unprofessional weakness. But out of the corner of her eye she saw that Falcon had turned away too.

CHAPTER 33

There was a knock on the door and a man carrying a clipboard with a map attached to it came into the office. Hannah recognised him as one of the detectives on the team.

"I've plotted the sightings to date, guv."

Mallory cleared a space on the desk and the detective put the board down. Then he pointed at the pins that were stuck into the map. They had large round tops with writing on them.

"The numbers on the pins refer to the dates of the sightings. Red pins are verified sightings. Which means we've checked the callers and they genuinely believe they've seen Devril. Blue pins are not verified because we can't get hold of the people who called them in. And we've filtered out the genuine nutters."

"Thanks, Dave. Hang around for a few minutes, will you."

Mallory arranged the position of the board so that everyone standing around the desk could see it. At once, Hannah was struck by a pattern in the pins. About two thirds of them were randomly scattered around various locations in Garton itself. But the remainder were all in the vicinity of a village about fifteen miles to the north.

"Now just look at that." Falcon pointed to the pins around the village. "According to the dates of the sightings, our man was in this location two days before we picked him up down by the docks." He leaned forward so he could read the name on the map. "Farnehamly. Now why does that name ring a bell?"

"It's an old village, built around a lake in a forest area. There's a large leisure centre there," Hannah replied. "And . . ."

She stopped as the internal phone on the desk rang.

Mallory picked up the receiver and held it to his ear. "Thank you. Bring him to my office." He put the phone down. "John Devril's just been brought in, and he's on his way here now."

"How do we play this?" Falcon asked.

Mallory thought for a moment. "To begin with, informally. We'll talk to him here without a tape. Might make him open up more. But if I suspect for one moment that he's holding anything back I'll formally charge him with obstructing a police investigation."

Falcon raised his eyebrows, and Mallory shrugged. "So it might not stick, but it could just frighten him into opening up."

A uniformed WPC brought John Devril to the office, and Mallory moved forward to shake his hand.

"Mr Devril, thank you for agreeing to talk to us. We just want to ask a few questions and we're happy to keep it informal if you are."

"Of course. I'm sorry I was away when the officers first called. We've been to see an old friend in the country. But I heard the press release on the radio. It didn't say so, but you suspect Peter of being the Toybreaker, don't you?"

Mallory looked at him, considering the best way to handle the direct question. In the end he opted to be direct himself.

"Yes, you're right. We suspect your brother of being the Toybreaker."

"I can't believe it. I just can't believe it. Not of Peter. He's as gentle as a lamb."

"Mr Devril," it was Hannah who answered him, "the man who is the Toybreaker is not your brother as you remember him. We think he's undergone a profound psychological change."

"And we need to find him before he acts again," Mallory came in.

"Before he acts again. Is that a euphemism, Chief Superintendent? Do you mean before he kills again?"

Mallory looked at him once more. "There's information about this case that cannot be released to the public yet. And God knows, there's enough speculation about the fate of those kids floating around. So, I'll deny I said this to you. But we know that all the kids who were abducted have died. So yes, I mean before he kills again."

John Devril collapsed into one of the chairs and put his head in his hands. He stayed like that for a long time, his shoulders shaking. Then finally he looked up, his eyes red.

"I'll do anything I can to stop this."

"Thank you." Mallory let his breath out. "We need to find your brother and a number of sightings have been reported. Some of them are in Garton itself, which is reasonable because we know he's been in the city for some time. But there has also been a series of sightings around the village of Farnehamly. Can you think why?"

"Farnehamly? No. There's a leisure centre there, but I don't know that Peter has any connection to the place. Unless . . ."

"Unless what?" Falcon prompted him.

"Some friends of our parents have a holiday chalet there and Mum and Dad stayed in it sometimes. I once went to see them there. Maybe the owners let Peter use it. When I was working abroad perhaps."

"Can you find out? Now, please," Falcon sounded excited.

"I can phone the owners, but I'll need a telephone directory because I don't know the number."

"Come with me." Falcon took him away.

When the two of them came back a few minutes later, Falcon was smiling. "It's our lucky day — for a change. Apparently Peter Devril and his family have stayed in the chalet for their holidays for the last two summers. It's in the woods not far from the lake, and according to the owners, Peter and Jason, loved it there. They could walk, ride their bikes along nature trails, swim and picnic in the area. It seems they used to look forward to the holiday for months."

"Is the chalet only used in the summer?" Mallory asked John Devril.

"I don't know the terms of the lease, but I do know that my parents' friends used it at different times of the year."

"How isolated is it?"

"There are other chalets around, but it's screened off by trees for privacy."

"So someone could be in there without anyone else knowing?"

"Yes, I suppose they could."

"Mr Devril, I think you'd better take us there."

Just then the internal phone rang again. Falcon reached over and picked up the receiver, then handed then handed it straight to Mallory.

There was silence in the office as Mallory listened. Then slowly and deliberately he replaced the receiver on the cradle.

"That was the press office. Another message from the Toybreaker. Only this time he's gone public and sent it directly to the press. And he's threatening a massacre of innocent children. Something about 'a fiery furnace for the vengeance of God.'"

CHAPTER 34

Cathleen Foster remained standing in what was rapidly becoming an overcrowded office. She was in her late twenties, with an oval-shaped face and blond hair that had obviously been styled. But she was severely dressed in a dark business suit, and there was a no-nonsense air about her that suggested the seasoned professional.

She handed Mallory a sheet of paper. "This was faxed in from the editor of the *Garton Evening News*. It's a copy of a letter received by the paper at two fifteen today. The editor's keeping the original for now, and at my suggestion it's been placed in a plastic bag to protect it. It's probably too late because several people have already handled it, but it was the best I could do." Her voice sounded hoarse.

"Thanks, Cathleen. By the way, this is Hannah Nightingale, the profiler on the case."

"Hi." Cathleen Foster extended her hand. "I'm sorry I wasn't around when you joined the team, but I've been off with a bad dose of the flu."

Hannah shook her hand. "There's a lot of it about. You OK now?"

"No." She grinned ruefully. "But this is the biggest case I'm ever likely to handle and I felt I should be on the spot."

"Shit." The short expletive from Mallory cut short their conversation.

He handed the fax to Falcon who held it so that Hannah could also see it. The message was composed of letters of different sizes and typefaces that looked as if they'd been cut from a newspaper. Just like the first message.

> *The darkness is upon the land and many of the little children will perish this time in the fiery furnace, for remember the words of the Lord thy God — Vengeance is mine. I will repay.*

"Can I have a closer look, please?" Hannah held out her hand. Without a word Mallory passed her the fax, and she read through it again.

"A strange mixture of religious misquotes. Probably bits he picked up from Carol Devril, and didn't remember properly. I think this is genuine."

"I agree." Mallory nodded. "But what's the point of sending it?"

"The first letter, the one about leaving a sign at the museum, was to torment the police. This one is to frighten the public. To spread fear. He knows by now we will have found the bodies at the old asylum. But he'll also know we've kept it from the media in case it causes panic. So he's generating his own kind of fear. And he talks about a 'vengeful God,' which means he's admitting that this whole thing's about revenge. Particularly the quote 'I will repay.' No secrets anymore. We're approaching the end game now. He's got something planned, and it must be something big because he mentions many little children."

"So what line do we take with the editor?" Cathleen Foster asked.

"Jesus, we can't afford the kind of panic this would generate among the public." It was Falcon who answered.

"I agree," Mallory almost snarled the words. "Promise the editor an inside scoop on the whole Toybreaker case when it's over. He can sell in on to the nationals then. Promise him that. Promise him anything. Just get him to hold back on the letter. Can you do that?"

"He's a pretty socially responsible guy, and I'm sure I can persuade him to play ball, Chief Superintendent. At least for the moment."

"Thanks." Mallory turned to Falcon. "We need to set up a team to check Farnehamly. And we need it now, which means we don't have time for the sort of detailed planning an operation of this kind requires. I'm not happy with that, but we've no choice."

"Get county in?"

Mallory shook his head. "Definitely not. I don't want the bumpkins blundering around. We'll liaise with them, of course, let them know we're operating on their patch. But there's no rush for that. The priority is starting things moving. Get an armed response team and two helicopters standing by. The commander of the team can decide the size of the squad that goes, but it's limited by the number the choppers can take."

"Who goes besides the cavalry?"

"Minimum presence at this time. You, me and Mr Devril, because he can take us directly to the chalet. And Hannah because if we find the Toybreaker, we might just need help handling him."

Mallory was turning away when Cathleen Foster caught his arm. "Did you say you were going to Farnehamly?"

"Farnehamly?" Mallory seemed to have forgotten she was there. "Yes, why?"

"It's just that the festival's on now."

"Festival? What festival?" Mallory was trying to curb his impatience at what he obviously saw as a distraction.

"The Fire Festival. It's held once every ten years to commemorate the battle when the villagers fought off the Vikings."

"Hold it there." Falcon heard an alarm bell ringing in his mind. "A fire festival, you say?"

"Yes. I know about it because I was a junior reporter on the local rag the last time it was held."

"You thinking what I'm thinking?" Mallory looked at Falcon.

"The Toybreaker's threatening a grand gesture. A gesture that involves a fiery furnace. I thought it was just symbolism when I read the note. But now he's been spotted at a place that's holding a fire festival. I'd say there was too many coincidences there."

"A damned sight too many." Mallory turned to Cathleen Foster. "So tell us about this festival."

"Well, it seems that towards the end of the ninth century the coastal area around Farnehamly was raided by Vikings from Ireland. At that time it was a small village on the edge of a lake. There was an island in the lake that had an monastic settlement on it that had been founded by one of the wandering Celtic saints. In this particular Viking attack the villages abandoned their houses and sailed to the island where they were sheltered by the monks. But the Vikings suspected that there were gold ornaments at the monastery and they were determined to get hold of them. They were sailors themselves, of course, and their longships were designed so that they could be hauled over the ground. So they brought one of them to the lake and sailed for the island. Once it was seen, the abbot from the monastery boarded one of the village ships and went out to meet them, appealing for them to spare the island which he said was a holy place. The Vikings refused, but the village boat had been made into a fire ship and it crashed into the longship setting it afire and killing the raiders on board. According to the legend the abbot was last seen in the prow of the fire ship as it approached the Viking vessel."

"So what happens at the festival?"

"As I said, it's a commemoration of the battle. But I think the actual details differ each time it's held."

"And when's it being held?"

"Today. Or, this evening rather."

"Shit." The expletive again. "Who's in charge of the proceedings?"

"It's run by a committee from County Hall, but the person in overall charge is the festival director."

Mallory was thinking on his feet. "A change of priorities." He faced Falcon. "Time's too compressed now, and it's vital we set up a radio network. I need to start talking to people even before we get in the air, and that means bringing in a communications team. And bring forward the liaison with county."

"I'll see to it straight away."

"So let's move." Mallory sounded more sure of himself now the action was about to start. "And just hope to God we can stop the Toybreaker this time. Before he carries out his 'massacre of the innocents.'"

CHAPTER 35

It was six in the evening by the time the helicopter landed by the side of the lake.

As soon as he'd learned about the festival, Mallory had abandoned any ideas of keeping the local police on the sidelines, and following the intervention of the chief constable a communications link had been set up between the Garton and county forces. As part of the set-up, Mallory was to liaise directly with a county chief superintendent who had established a base in a caravan that was already being used as the command centre for the officers policing the festival.

The problem that faced them all was time, and after an initial discussion between the two senior officers it was decided to use a county armed response team to reconnoitre the chalet that John Devril had identified. The results came over the radio network just as the helicopter was about to land. There was no one in the chalet, but there were signs that it had been occupied recently. And one of the items found was a newspaper with sections cut out of it where individual letters had been removed.

Mallory had asked county to have the festival director on standby, and as soon as the helicopter landed Mallory,

Hannah, Falcon and John Devril were driven to the command centre. A uniformed chief superintendent was waiting for them, with a civilian standing next to him. The officer shook hands with Mallory.

"Bill Macklin. We've not met, but I'm happy to cooperate every way I can." He indicated the man next to him. "This is the festival director."

He was middle-aged, dressed in faded wax jacket and corduroys. A tall and rangy man, with the ruddy complexion of someone used to working outside. He exuded an impression of unflappable reliability.

"Craig Lawson." He shook Mallory's hand. "I gather you people think there's a dangerous madman on the loose around here. So how can I help."

Mentally, Mallory said a prayer of thanks. Lawson was obviously a man of action who didn't go in for endless talk and didn't need lengthy explanations.

"First, I need to know the programme for this evening."

"Right. There've been a series of events during the day, but the main attraction is the fire ceremony itself which is about to kick off soon."

"What exactly happens?"

"Essentially, a Viking longship leaves the lakeside and sails towards the island. When it's halfway across, a Celtic ship leaves the island with an effigy of the abbot standing in the bows. As it closes with the Viking vessel the Celtic ship is set on fire by remote control and then the two ships crash and eventually sink."

"How does the ceremony actually work?"

"It's all set up by a firm from London that specialise in historical pageants. They're not cheap, but we got a European Union grant for the festival. And as part of the deal we have to involve the public to a greater extent than in the past. We've run a series of mobile exhibitions in town centres and schools, and there's been various wild life awareness events associated with the festival. But today's the main day and we've been building up to the climax since this morning."

"The climax. What does that involve?"

"The pageant on the lake. It starts off with the mock battle for the island, then there's a major firework display. There are grandstands on the lakeside for those with tickets, and the rest can watch from specially designated areas. Oh yes, and children from the local primary schools can see it all first hand. From an Edwardian paddle steamer out on the lake. It's a special treat for them. They're all dressed in Edwardian clothes and there's old style entertainment for them. Clowns, jugglers, that sort of thing. That's another innovation this year as well."

"How many children are on the steamer?"

"Forty-five, plus teachers."

"Oh, Christ." Falcon hit the table with the edge of his hand. "The 'massacre of the innocents.' We have to stop that steamer sailing."

"It's too late." Lawson's voice sounded bleak. "She left the landing stage ten minutes ago."

CHAPTER 36

The launch raced across the surface of the lake. It belonged to the local boat club which was providing safety and rescue marshals for the festival, but it showed no lights now as it approached the stern of the paddle steamer.

Mallory had already contacted the captain of the vessel over the radio and explained that the children on the ship were in danger. The ship had already stopped at the position where the children would be able to observe the fire fight, and the captain had wanted to get back underway and head for the shore at once. But Mallory told him there was every chance that a maniac was on board who might panic if he thought the ship was returning to shore. Instead, Mallory said that a police unit was about to board the ship and that the operation must be carried out in secret. There was no time to devise a foolproof plan, but after some discussion the captain suggested that they approach the paddle steamer from the stern where they could board through a section of rail which could be opened.

All the party in the launch, including Mallory, Falcon and Hannah, were dressed in body armour under dark blue flak jackets. For rapid identification, the jackets had a broad strip of material that would fluoresce in the beam of a torch. On their heads they wore baseball caps with POLICE stencilled on them in bright white letters. Five of the officers from the armed response unit were carrying Heckler and Koch MP5 sub-machine guns, but the sixth had a sniper rifle with a night sight. In addition every member of the team carried tear gas and stun grenades. The men were linked by a state-of-the-art communication system that Mallory and Falcon were also plugged into via throat microphones and earphones.

As the launch drew close to the stationary vessel, two of the paddle-steamer's crew released a section of the stern rail which swung open. The launch turned in an arc to close with the steamer and one by one the party leapt the gap, helped onto the deck by the crew members. The members of the armed response unit went first, followed by Hannah and then Falcon.

When they were safely on board Mallory joined them and the section of rail was clipped back into place behind him. On his signal, the launch pulled away and was soon lost in the night.

One of the ship's officers was standing in the shadows and he came forward to meet Mallory. He was wearing the uniform of an Edwardian mercantile officer.

"Zac Davies, first officer." He shook Mallory's hand and looked at the members of the armed response unit. "Bloody hell, you boys don't play games."

"No game, Zac. It's just possible there's a madman on this ship," Mallory sounded grim.

"And the old man tells me he intends to harm the kids."

"Yes, we have good reason to believe that. So what's happening on board at the moment?"

"The kids are all out on the fore deck for the entertainment. Look." He pulled a folded sheet of paper from one of his pockets, opened it out, and spread it over the top of a locker.

"This is a plan of the paddle steamer."

Mallory unclipped a torch from his belt and shone it on the drawing as the party gathered around him.

"This is a lake steamer, and as you can see the paddles and the bridge house are set back. The reason for that is to give the passengers as much open deck space as possible, and we're using that space for the entertainment. The kids are all sitting in rows on the deck and we've built a stage in the bows. It's a real stage, a facsimile of an Edwardian music hall with full lighting. The works."

"And what sort of entertainment are you putting on?" Mallory asked him.

"It's been set up by the people who are running the pageant. I've got a programme here somewhere." He rummaged in one of the pockets of his elaborate uniform and pulled out another sheet of paper. He gave it to Mallory, who held it in the beam of the torch.

The programme was printed on thick yellow paper. On the front under the heading *Farnehamly Fire Festival* there was an engraving of the paddle steamer and below it a list of events, starting with 'Mr David — The original Punch and Judy Man,' and ending with a puppet show by a local theatre group.

"There." Zac Davies pointed to the last item. "The puppets are on now, and the show should be ending soon. So the kids can watch the fire ships."

Puppets.

The shock hit Mallory. "Can you take us to see the entertainment, somewhere we can watch without being seen."

"No problem."

They followed Zac Davies along the deck until they were in the shadow of the bridge house. Then he lead then up steeply angled steps and they came out on the starboard bridge wing behind a polished brass rail. Mallory was aware of figures in the glass-fronted cabin in the centre of the bridge, but his eyes were fixed on the scene ahead of him.

The deck lights had been switched off, but he was aware of the rows of children sitting under a blue and white stripped awning facing the brightly lit stage ahead of them. For the moment they were quiet, their eyes fixed on the stage. Their attention held by the life-sized puppet that was slowly dancing across the boards.

And in that instant Mallory knew this was no wild goose chase. The figure the children were watching was a clown. Just like those found at the crime scenes. But this one was much larger.

The final creation of the Toybreaker.

CHAPTER 37

Mallory pulled his team back off the bridge, and gathered them together in the shadows by the side of the ladder.

"Who's in charge of the entertainment on the ship?" he asked Zac Davies.

"Mike Conron, the stage manager."

"Can you bring him here, please. We need to know how our man got onto the stage."

Zac disappeared and Mallory pulled the team closer around him.

"OK, we know the Toybreaker's started to run the show. That's his puppet out there. But the priority at the moment has to be the children, which means we take out the Toybreaker if we have to. Problem is, at the moment we don't have a sighting of him because he's controlling the puppet from some part of the stage we can't see."

He gestured to the inspector in command of the armed response unit. "Ken, put your sniper on the bridge. He'll have a clear line of sight to the stage from there."

At that moment Zac Davies returned. "Mike Conron's dead. I went to the cabin the performers used for changing, and when I got there the act that was supposed to be on the stage now were standing around waiting. They knew nothing about the new act and they didn't know where the stage manager was either. Then I found his body pushed under a pile of curtains in a corner of the cabin."

Mallory looked at Hannah. "He killed the stage manager. Does that mean he's desperate?"

She shook her head. "No, I'm very much afraid it means he doesn't care anymore. We really are in the end game now."

"And you think he intends to harm the children?" Falcon asked.

"Yes. I believe his mind's gone over the edge. He wants to take his final revenge on those children, and he knows he'll go down with them. That's why he was prepared to kill the stage manager."

"But what the hell does he intend to do?" The frustration was plain in Falcon's voice. He felt helpless, and it was obviously getting to him. But he forced himself to concentrate.

"Zac, there are forty-five kid out there, right?"

"Right."

"So if Peter Devril intends to kill them all he must have something drastic planned. Something that will affect the whole ship. Any ideas what he might have set up?" He turned back to Zac Davies.

"I'd narrow it down to two alternatives. Sink the ship, or start a major fire."

"I'd go for fire," Hannah said. "His message said the children would perish in the flames."

"OK," Falcon agreed. "So how would he start the fire so it would spread quickly enough to engulf the ship?"

"One thing we've learned as this case progressed is not to underestimate the Toybreaker," Mallory said. "Simple he may be, but he's got some sort of instinctive cunning in his make-up. My guess is he'll use explosives to start the fire."

No one argued with him.

"OK, next question. Where would he have set the explosives Zac?"

"I don't know, but probably somewhere around the deck where the children are sitting. That's where I'd position them anyway. I can get the crew to run a quick search, if you like."

"Won't they be seen from the stage?"

"Not if they keep to the shadows around the edge of the deck. It won't be a thorough search, but it might turn up something."

"Give it a shot, but tell your men to stay hidden."

Zac Davies disappeared round the side of the bridge.

"We can't risk forcing the Toybreaker's hand. And if we try to move the children that's just what we'll be doing." Mallory was thinking out loud. "But we can't just sit back until he's finished his act either. Because that could be too late. We have to take him out before he can make his move. Which means making him show himself."

A sudden roar of childish laughter and a loud burst of applause came from the deck ahead of them. Hannah wondered whether the act was reaching its climax.

Zac Davies came round the bridge and approached Mallory. He was panting, and had to force the words out.

"We know how he plans to set fire to the ship. He's stored plastic containers of petrol in the lifeboats under the canvas covers, and he's set a line of explosives through them. It'll be an inferno when it all goes up, and the kids will be trapped in a ring of fire."

CHAPTER 38

"How does he intend to trigger the explosives?" Mallory shot the question at Zac Davies.

"I don't know, but there's wiring running along the deck into small metal boxes taped to each petrol container."

"A sophisticated system. So how the hell did Peter Devril manage to rig it up?" Falcon asked, but before anyone could reply he answered the question himself. "Of course, Days Long Ago. When we checked him out with the company, one of the things the girl from personnel told us was that they designed remote controlled firework displays."

"I said we shouldn't underestimate him," Mallory's voice was soft. "There are two things he learned at Days Long Ago. How to rig-up firework displays, and how to run puppet shows. And he's using both skills now. But where did he get the material to set up the explosions from?"

"He probably went back to Days Long Ago and stole what he needed," Falcon replied." In any case, he's got the bloody ship wired up."

"But we know about it now," Zac Davies said.

"True," Falcon agreed. "And I don't think the system will be booby trapped with anything as sophisticated as say a tremor device. Because that would require skills Devril wouldn't have picked up. But we just can't take that risk that he hasn't rigged -up something cruder. And there's no time to bring in an explosive expert to check out the system either. So how do we play it?"

Mallory was quiet for a few moments, an island of calm while he forced himself to think.

"Zac, if we can get the children back here safely, is it possible to bring another ship alongside and transfer them on to it?"

"It's very calm on the lake tonight so there'd be little movement. But they're only kids and many of them will be frightened of water. Which means trying to move them in a confined space could cause a panic. So, yes, it's possible, but it's bloody risky."

Mallory nodded. "I agree. But not half as risky as getting trapped on the deck of a burning ship with their escape cut off by the flames."

Zac Davies didn't waste time arguing with the logic of that. "We could use *The Mammoth.* If any vessel could do it, she could."

"What's *The Mammoth?*" Mallory asked him.

"She's a broad beamed steam tug with a powerful engine. But more important, the bridge house is forward and the after deck space is flat with no obstructions. That'll offer a reasonably stable platform for the kids. And it has a safety rail around it."

"But how long will it take to get a crew on board and get her ready to sail?"

"No time at all. That's the beauty of it. In addition to the rescue launches, *The Mammoth's* on standby with a full head of steam up ready to tackle major emergencies. It's all part of the safety precautions the insurance people insisted on."

"Right. We can't risk attempting to deactivate the petrol bombs. So there's no alternative, we have to try to evacuate the children. I'll take full responsibility for the decision and I'll get onto Chief Superintendent Macklan to arrange for the tug to come to the ship. But you're the seaman, Zac, and I'd like you to liaise with the skipper of the tug and be in charge of the exchange itself."

"No problem. I'll call up the bridge and let the old man know what's happening here, then I'll contact the tug and work out the safest way of coming alongside and transferring the children."

Mallory turned to Falcon. "You talk to the teachers. Find some way of getting one of them off the deck and let them know what's happening. Tell them about the explosives and stress that the kids are in extreme danger. Then get that teacher to explain the situation to the rest of them. It won't look suspicious if a teacher is seen walking about the deck speaking to other teachers. Now, there's just one more problem."

"Just one?" Falcon grunted.

"Well, only one I'm prepared to think about. Otherwise, I might just become the tiniest bit hysterical."

"And what is this problem, guv?"

"How long will it take for the tug to get here?" Mallory asked Zac Davies.

Davies thought for a moment. "Steam's up, crew's on standby. Allowing for time to pull away from the landing stage and get up to speed, I'd say no more than about five minutes to reach us at this position. Then we've got to add on time to secure the two vessels together. Say another five minutes. Then however long it takes to make the transfer itself."

"OK, so allow another five minutes for Macklan to set it all up. We're talking fifteen, maybe twenty minutes, before we're even ready to start the evacuation. So we've got to buy time. Somehow, we've got to keep Peter Devril occupied while all this is happening."

"I think I know how we can do that," Hannah suddenly sounded excited. "The tape. The Christmas tape of him and his boy. I've got it with me in my handbag. Can we play it over the ship's public address system?"

"No problem." Zac Davies held out his hand. "Give it to me and I'll get it up to the bridge. That way I can brief the old man in person and use the main radio to contact *The Mammoth.*"

"Chief Inspector Falcon brought spare radio sets," Mallory said. "He'll let you have one and show you how to work it. And when you get to the bridge keep me informed of developments at every stage."

* * *

A few minutes later the public address system burst into life with a loud crackle of static. A young voice was heard giggling, then it began to sing and the words of *Away in a Manger* floated on the night air. There was a sudden silence as the children on the deck heard the familiar carol. Then, one by one, the tiny voices began to join in thinking it was part of the entertainment.

As Hannah listened she thought there was something hauntingly sweet in the soft resonance of the words of that gentle carol as they echoed around the steamer.

"Look." Falcon pointed at the stage.

The puppet was still now, frozen with its arms raised in the air. As if it was listening to the children sing.

The carol came to an end and the voices of the children faded away. Then the conversation between the man and the boy started. They were building the manger. This was something the children on the deck knew about and there was an excited babble of voices as they listened.

"NO." The voice crashed out from the stage. A great roar of sound that drowned out the words from the tape, and the children became silent again.

Hannah looked around the side of the bridge housing at the stage, and at that moment the voice on the tape began to sign *Once in Royal David's City.* Only this time the children didn't join in, sensing that something was wrong. Something they didn't understand.

"STOP." The voice came again, higher pitched now.

"We're losing him." Hannah gazed forward into the night.

"Is there anything else we can do?" Mallory was beginning to sound desperate.

Hannah hesitated. She knew that Peter Devril had to be stopped before he harmed the children. And as long as he stayed hidden, out of sight of the sniper, there was only one way to protect the little ones.

She would have to face her own nightmares.

"Let me talk to Peter Devril," she said to Mallory.

"Won't that make him feel threatened?"

"Not if I take it slowly."

There was something in her voice that Mallory picked up. "You're not sure, are you?"

She shook her head. "No, I'm not sure. I just don't know how far his mind's fragmented. That last cry sounded so off centre. So remote. I think he's just about cut off from all reality, and when that finally happens he'll become totally unpredictable. At the moment we've got two chances to save the children. Either we persuade Peter Devril to let them go, or we buy enough time to evacuate them. I can explore both of those possibilities. But one thing's for sure, if I don't try now it will be too late to save the children."

Mallory looked over the side and picked out the shadow of the tug coming up through the night. Everything was starting to fall into place. But if Peter Devril was becoming as unpredictable as Hannah thought he was, it would all unravel if he finally lost it and the ship would go up in a fireball.

"Go on then, try and talk to him. We'll fit you up with a radio set and keep you in touch with how the evacuation's proceeding. And the minute the situation with Devril looks as if it's going pear-shaped, get back here."

Mallory knew only too well that it wouldn't make much difference where she was if the ship went up. But he kept the thought to himself.

CHAPTER 39

For a moment she was rooted to the spot. Trapped there by a deep seated feeling of inadequacy.

Inadequacy and fear.

A normal interview session with a patient like Peter Devril would require hours of detailed planning and would take place under carefully regulated conditions. But there was no time for any of that, and Hannah knew she would have to improvise. Quickly, she mapped out a way to approach the problem. First, she would try to reclaim Peter Devril's own personality and reason with him. But by now any faint trace of the old Peter Devril would be hidden deep in the shadows of his mind, and she knew it would not be given up easily. So if she failed to reclaim him she would have to fall back on buying time. Which meant confronting the Toybreaker head on.

And that was what made her afraid.

The thought of a one-to-one confrontation with Peter Devril brought memories of the Explorer flooding back. Images of the gibbering shell of a man left behind when she'd made him face his demons. But most of all, she thought of how the evil she'd released had threatened her own sanity.

For a moment she seemed trapped there, afraid to face the 'thing' that was waiting on the stage. Then, finally, she forced herself to move forward. She kept to the edge of the deck and walked past the rows of children, silent now and apprehensive. She stopped at the front of the stage and peered into the darkness, trying to trace back the wires controlling the puppet. She thought she could see the faint outline of a small balcony raised above the stage, but it was too dark to make out the details. She looked up at the puppet. It was still frozen in its pose, although the tape had run out now.

"Peter," she called out softly. "Can you hear me?"

There was a long pause, then a voice came from the darkness at the back of the stage.

"Who are you?" The tone was oddly scratchy, but otherwise the voice seemed normal enough, and for a moment Hannah dared to hope it belonged to Peter Devril and not the Toybreaker.

"My name's Hannah. Hannah Nightingale, and I've come to help you."

"Help me? How?"

"I'm a doctor, Peter, and I can help you if you'll let me." She was suddenly conscious of how ludicrous the situation was. Trying to carry out a mental health consultation on the deck of a paddle steamer in the darkness with a patient she couldn't see.

"I don't need a doctor." The tone of voice changed suddenly. Deeper this time, less scratchy. "I'm not sick." The puppet gave a sudden jerk and Hannah jumped back.

It was clear to her then that the Toybreaker could take over at will. He was playing with her, and he would continue playing with her for as long as he held the upper hand. There was only one way forward. She would have to be more confrontational. It was a high risk strategy so early in the interview, but she felt she had little choice.

"I didn't say you were sick, Peter. But I think you need help."

"Why?"

"Because you want to harm the little children watching your puppet show. Don't you like children?"

There was another long pause. "Yes." It was a tortured gasp. "I like children." Peter Devril was coming back.

"You liked Jason, didn't you?" she pressed on.

"Jason." He drew the word out in a long sigh. "I loved Jason. We used to do things together." Silence now, and Hannah could hear him breathing somewhere above her. "Jason was special."

Still Peter Devril. Perhaps she really was beginning to flush him out. "Peter, can you tell me something?"

"What?"

"It's about your wife Carol."

There was another pause, shorter this time. "She's dead. Carol's dead."

"How did she die, Peter?"

"I killed her."

No hesitation now. And no pretence. Peter Devril had killed her, and he wasn't bothering to hide it.

"Why did you take her life away from her?"

"She was going to kill Jason." The words were like a hacking cough now. "And I couldn't let her harm him, could I?" It was the pitiful plea of a child.

Hannah held her breath. She'd done it. Jason was the key that had unlocked Peter Devril's mind and released the trace of his original personality that had been sheltering there. This was the one opportunity she would have to persuade Peter Devril to free the children. But it was a fragile moment, and if she got it wrong there would be no second chance. For the sake of the children she had to move slowly.

"No, you couldn't let her harm Jason." She spoke softly, her tone conciliatory. "I can understand that. So what happened?"

"I killed her then buried the body. But she didn't know it was me who did it."

"What do you mean, she didn't know it was you?"

"I stopped her seeing me." His tone was sly, as if he'd done something very cleaver.

The metal skewers, Hannah thought. God, how she must have suffered when he'd blinded her with them. No one should have to go through that. Not even the worst kind of child killer like Carol Devril.

"What did you do after you'd buried the body?" Hannah was having to fight to keep her own voice under control. To keep him from sensing the revulsion she felt.

"I went back to see Jason."

"Was someone looking after him in the house?"

"Yes, the girl from next door."

"Was that the day of the fire, Peter?"

"Yes, when I got back the house was on fire, and Jason and the other girl were dead."

Another piece of the jigsaw.

"So why did you say the other body was Carol's."

"So nobody would know I'd killed her."

"What happened after the fire?" Hannah asked. But there was no answer this time, and the silence seemed to stretch out into an eternity.

Suddenly her ear piece crackled and she heard Mallory's voice, metallic and low. "Evacuation proceeding, but not complete. Keep suspect talking."

All very well, she thought, but Peter Devril was slipping away. Desperate now, she tried to bring him back.

"Peter, think about Jason. About all the lovely times you had together. Can you still remember them?"

"Yes." He was back.

"Then will you help the children on the boat? You don't want to harm them do you?"

A long silence.

"They must pay." The voice was different. Commanding. Powerful. "Jason must be avenged."

Peter Devril had gone. There was no way now he could be persuaded to release the children. The only chance left for them was to win time to complete the evacuation and get clear of the ship before it went up in an inferno. And Hannah had to buy that time. Which meant moving into that uncharted territory she'd told Mallory about.

She would have to enter the realm of the Toybreaker.

CHAPTER 40

"You wanted revenge, didn't you? Revenge for what happened to Jason?"

"Why did Jason die? Why was he taken away from me? It wasn't right." The voice was booming now.

"So you wanted to take your revenge by killing other children. By taking them away from their parents. And you did kill those babies, didn't you? Didn't you? It was you, wasn't it?" It was full confrontation now. And it paid off.

There was a sudden change in the air, a flutter in pressure that pressed outwards from the stage. And a cold, cold mist seemed to wrap itself around the deck. Then the voice came.

"I killed them. I did it."

It was a different voice this time. A parody of a woman's voice, a high-pitched resonant snarl. An inhuman, grotesque sound. And as she heard it, Hannah felt the terror engulf her. This was something dark, something she didn't understand, and for a moment she seemed to freeze. Afraid she was facing some form of evil possession.

Then a part of her mind freed itself, a narrow confined space where she could still function as a professional. And as she reasserted herself, the revelation came like a shaft of light. Now, at last, she understood the mechanics of how the gentle, caring Peter Devril had become the Toybreaker. And with that realisation the fear that was holding her in thrall evaporated.

"Who are you?" Hannah asked the question, although she already certain of the answer.

"*Carol. I am Carol.*"

The final piece of the puzzle. Peter Devril wasn't possessed. This was something he'd brought on himself.

Hannah could see it all then. Peter Devril had needed to exact revenge, but he could never kill little children. So he'd deliberately assumed the personality of his dead wife. Pretending to himself that she was the one who was killing the children. At first, he'd only needed to be Carol when he carried out the abductions and he'd been in control then, able to switch between his own personality and that of the alien he'd brought in. But Hannah guessed that as he kept on killing, his guilt must have increased, forcing a battle to rage within him. Until the only way he could cope was to shut out his own personality more and more. So that in the end only a few remnants were left. But now, by turning the screw on Peter Devril, Hannah had driven out those remnants by finally making him admit he was Carol. With the remnants gone, he was no longer able to switch back to his own personality. And it was Hannah's fault.

She had forced the situation until it reached this point, and if the children were killed she would forever bear the guilt, which left her with no choice. If she wanted to buy more time she had to take the 'thing' on in battle. The fate of the children depended on who won that battle, and if she was to emerge the victor Hannah knew she had to break through the barriers and reach into the far corners of Peter Devril's mind to make him confront what he had done. The Explorer all over again.

But there was nothing else she could do, and everything now depended on her skill as an interrogator.

"Carol, why do you want to harm little children?"

"*Sod off, bitch. Go back where you belong. In the sewers.*"

"You have no right to be here."

"*What do you know, shithead?*"

"I know you're harming Peter."

"*Harming him. How little you know, stupid bitch. Peter wants me here.*"

"But he hates you," Hannah deliberately raised her voice. "He killed you, didn't he? He killed you?"

"*Bitch, bitch, bitch, bitch, bitch, bitch.*" The words flooded out in a stream of bitter vitriol.

"If he wants you here, why did he kill you, Carol?"

"*Shut up.*"

"Go away and stop Peter suffering. Leave him now."

"*You think you know everything, don't you, bitch? But you don't. You don't know why Peter wants me inside him.*" The tone was sneering now. Dismissive.

"So tell me. Why does he want you to take him over?"

There was another silence, and it seemed to go on forever this time. Then it was shattered.

"*Because I am death.*" The words were screamed out.

And Hannah realised what had happened, and she knew she'd been wrong. Peter Devril *had* found a way of switching back to his own personality. Somehow he'd managed to concentrate all the hatred in his tortured soul into one malevolent core of pure evil. It was the moment of cathexis, the concentration of mental energy into a single channel, and it had served to cleanse his mind. But it had brought its own danger with it.

As the scream faded to an echo a deep silence engulfed the ship, and even the noise of the waves lapping against the hull seemed faint and far away. Then it came. A long drawn-out wail of despair.

Peter Devril had finally realised what he'd done. He knew that he was the Toybreaker. And suddenly the puppet began to move again, but in sharp jerks this time.

The end was very near now.

CHAPTER 41

Hannah swung round and looked back. In the half-light she could see the deck was almost empty, and she began to run towards the stern. Behind the bridge housing she could see a corridor of people, men from the armed response unit, members of the paddle steamer's crew and women she assumed were teachers, guiding the last of the children towards a gap in the rail where another vessel was drawn up alongside the paddle steamer. At the end of the line Zac Davies lifted a young girl and swung her across to a man on the other vessel.

Hannah looked around and saw Mallory standing in the shadows below the bridge. He was watching, but he made no attempt to interfere. His job was done and it was up to others now. Hannah moved forward until she was standing next to him.

"It's finished. God knows what he'll do now."

Mallory glanced across the deck space. "Three more children. Then we have to cast off and get the tug clear. We still need more time."

Hannah looked round the side of the bridge housing at the stage. It was a bizarre sight as the puppet continued to perform its dance in the silence of the abandoned deck.

The movements were becoming more frenzied, a mad rhythm in which the marionette cavorted back and forward across the stage in wild abandon.

'What was Peter Devril doing?' Hannah wondered. 'Why was he delaying setting off the explosives?'

Then it started again. The wailing sound that came from behind the stage. And suddenly she knew the purpose of the puppet dance.

In the shell of his mind Peter Devril was still struggling to come to terms with the terrible knowledge that he was the Toybreaker. It had created chaos within him and the puppet, a totem smashed in anger at the crime scenes, had now become the symbol of the turmoil raging inside him.

The turmoil of the final battle.

Hannah looked at the waters around the paddle steamer. "There." She pointed beyond the bows. They'd been so engrossed in the drama being played out on the ship that they'd forgotten about the pageant unfolding on the lake.

Off the bows of the paddle steamer two vessels were approaching each other. One was a Viking longboat. There were two spotlights on board; one positioned to illuminate the row of brightly painted round shields in the bulwarks above the line of oars, and the other directed onto the square red and white striped sail at the central mast.

As it pushed through the water with the high prow carved in the form of a fierce dragon it looked like some great mythical beast torn from the old Norse Sagas. The other vessel was also a kind of clinker-built long ship, with a raised prow and stern. But this was a lake fishing boat, and although it carried a central mast and sail, it was much smaller that the Viking ship. Again, it was illuminated, but this time by a single light trained on a figure in a cape standing in the bows holding a shepherd's crook.

"What happens next?" Hannah asked Mallory.

"From what Craig Lawson said earlier the ships are steered by remote control, and as they close in the fire is started on the fishing boat. Then they crash and both catch fire and sink in the end."

"How much longer before the fire starts?"

Mallory shrugged. "I don't know, but the two ships are closing fast, and it can't be long now."

"Understood." Mallory lifted his hand in acknowledgement as Zac Davies signalled that the last of the children had been transferred to the tug. "Get the adults across." He pushed Hannah towards the rail, then spoke into his throat mike. "Mallory to bridge."

"Bridge." He heard Falcon's voice over the net.

"The children are on the tug. Abandon ship. Now."

He moved across the deck to where the section of rail had been removed and watched as the last of the teachers, then Hannah, crossed onto the other vessel. She was followed by the members of the armed response unit, and finally the crew of the paddle steamer. Zac Davies stayed behind, holding an axe to sever the ropes joining the two ships.

Mallory held back until Falcon and a tall man, presumably the captain, dressed like Zac Davies in an Edwardian naval uniform, came down the ladder from the bridge. He stood there for a moment, taking in the situation, then gestured for Mallory and Falcon to cross to the tug. The captain was traditionally the last to leave his ship and Mallory knew there was no time to argue about protocol. Instead he grabbed Falcon by the arm and they jumped across onto the deck of the other vessel.

The captain said something to Zac Davies who handed him the axe then crossed to the tug. For a moment the captain stood there, as if he was saying goodbye to his ship, then raised the axe and cut the ropes.

As the paddle steamer reared away he leapt across onto the deck of the tug, and the powerful engines pulled it away into the night.

* * *

As the paddle steamer drifted without power it was on a heading that would take it between the paths of the Viking long ship and the boat from the island.

Mallory stood in the bows of the tug watching, Hannah and Falcon by his side.

"What the hell's he waiting for?" Mallory spoke into the wind.

Hannah thought of the struggle raging in Peter Devril's mind. "I think he's trying to save the children. He believes they're still on the ship."

"What do you mean, he's trying to save the children? He's the one who's going to massacre them," Falcon sounded bewildered.

"No, he's not," Hannah said gently. "At least, not in his own mind."

"So he's fighting with himself," Falcon almost growled the words.

"He is now," she replied.

"What do you mean, now?" Falcon asked.

"Now that he acknowledges he's the Toybreaker."

"Jesus, this getting too deep for me. Do you mean that . . ."

"Look," Mallory cut him short, pointing to the paddle steamer. "In the bows."

The figure of a man appeared, caught in the festive lights illuminating the bows of the ship. For a moment, he looked back along the deck, then stood on the rail holding the flag staff to steady himself. Across the water, no more than ten yards away now, the boat from the island was about to cross the bows of the paddle steamer as it sliced through the water towards the Viking ship.

The man crouched on the rail, staring ahead, then dived to the side into the water. For a moment he disappeared from sight, lost in the choppy sea as the bow wave thrust forward.

"There." Falcon pointed, and as the boat from the island cut across the bows of the paddle steamer, a figure grabbed a rope hanging over the side and began to haul itself out of the water.

Once he was on board, the figure stood still, outlined in the beam of light directed at the bows. Even at that distance it was clear it was Peter Devril, his long hair blowing in the wind. He looked around, then made his way along the deck following the light into the bows. Once there, he climbed onto a platform and stood with his back against the model of the saint, his arms outstretched in the form of a cross.

"Bloody hell, the boat's going to catch fire. Can we stop it in time to . . ."

Mallory didn't finish the question because at that moment the boom of an explosion echoed across the surface of the lake and something in the body of the boat exploded in a rush of fire. It was a carefully designed stage effect and the flames, tall and blue tinged, began to march forward towards the bows.

"Jump. For God's sake. Before it's too late." Mallory heard himself shouting the words.

But Hannah put her hand on his arm. "He won't jump. For him the battle's over now. The fire fight's common knowledge, and he's well aware of what will happen to that boat. He can't face the future knowing what he did as the Toybreaker. That's why he's chosen to end it there."

"I still don't understand. Why has he left the paddle steamer?"

"Because he still doesn't know we got the children to safety. It was too dark on the deck for him to see what was happening. As far as he's concerned the children are still there."

"I see that. But why leave the ship?"

"Because he knows now that he's the Toybreaker, and he's afraid that the other personality will be strong enough to take over his mind again. So he's sacrificing himself to save the children. In the end, I suppose you could say that the good in Peter Devril prevailed." As Father David would say, she muttered under her breath.

The paddle steamer was well clear now, and the two boats that were the centre of the pageant were closing rapidly. As they did so, the fire in the boat from the village reached the bows and reared up. For a moment, the outline of Peter Devril's body was caught against the night sky.

Then, exactly on schedule, the figure of the saint burst into fire, a mass of flame that lit up the sky. And as it did so, it engulfed the body of Peter Devril.

At last the Toybreaker was at peace.

EPILOGUE

"So it's over, David."

"The Toybreaker's laid to rest, yes." Mallory bent down and released the lead from the dog's collar, and the animal bounded away across the course grass.

The two men were walking along a narrow dirt road that skirted the sweep of marshland dipping away towards the river. The sky was overcast, dark cloud banked up against the horizon and there was a hint of snow on the air.

"It was well done, David, and I'm sure there'll be a commendation or two for it later. Maybe even a medal."

"Just make sure Hannah Nightingale gets the recognition she deserves."

"Oh, don't worry about that. This investigation attracted a hell of a lot of bad publicity at times, and the police weren't exactly flavour of the month. Not with the Toybreaker holding the city in terror. So when we caught him there was a great sense of relief, but the real positive factor here was that we were able to save the lives of all those kids on the paddle steamer. And believe me, the press office will milk that for all it's worth, And Hannah will get her share of the credit. How's DCI Falcon by the way?" He changed the subject suddenly.

"Like the rest of us are after the successful end to a major operation. On a high at first because all the hard work's paid dividends, then reality sinks in and you find you're mentally shot. But right now getting back on an even keel isn't Gary's only problem."

"The mole?"

"Yes, the mole. He believes a lot of people still think he was the source that supplied his old man with the information. So despite the success of Toybreaker investigation, Gary still reckons his career's on hold, and that it will stay that way until the real mole is identified. At one time there were rumours that he was running an unofficial investigation of his own to flush out whoever it was. But the rumours seemed to stop when he was put on the Toybreaker case. Took up too much of his time, I suppose."

"Not just that. In fact, the mole was one of the reasons that I suggested we had this chat."

"Go on." Mallory stopped and turned to the other man.

"Falcon stopped running his own investigation because he was warned off. By me."

"And why should you have done that?"

"Because I didn't want the waters muddying. Look, David, what I'm going to tell you now is extremely confidential. So much so, that I would deny this conversation ever took place. But I think you have a right to know about the mole because it's related to Clayborn."

"You're saying Clayborn was the mole?"

"More than that, David. Much more. At the time of the racist incident with the chief constable, Clayborn was under investigation for corruption."

Mallory started to say something bit the other man held up his hand. "No questions. I'll tell you what I think you deserve to know. Then I'll tell you what I want you to pass on to Falcon. But that's it. The rest remains buried. Agreed?"

"Agreed."

"There'd been suspicions for some time that Clayborn was tied in with a drug-dealing ring in the city. Suspicions that received a strong boost when the undercover DS was killed and the investigation into the ring was called off."

"Christ, you mean Clayborn was deliberately responsible for the death of that officer?"

"I said no questions, David." The words were snapped at him. "That DS was one of our own, I know that. His death was tragic, particularly the manner in which he was killed, and I'd do anything to bring his murderer to justice. But take my word for it, there's no point in opening that old wound. The trail's dead. Right."

"Right." Mallory had enough respect for the other man to know he was telling the truth.

"So no more interruptions, whatever crawls out from under this particular stone."

"No more questions."

"Good. Now, like I said, there was a suspicion that Clayborn was on the take. But we still didn't have enough to move in on him, even after the death of the DS. Then I received an anonymous gift in the mail. A small section of video tape that showed Clayborn in the company of a known gang boss at what looked like a party somewhere. Not conclusive evidence of corruption in itself, but enough for me to initiate the investigation into Clayborn after discussions with Steve Morton, the then chief constable. It had to be done in secret, because if Clayborn knew he was under the microscope he could cover his tracks. Anyway, following official protocol an outside team was brought in to run the investigation. Unfortunately, it never really got off the ground. Nothing but brick walls. Even the video tape wouldn't stand up on its own because a good lawyer — and if charges were laid against him Clayborn would get the best — would simply say that the two men just happened to be at the same party along with many other people. And when it finally became evident that we were not going to be able to prove that Clayborn was associated with criminal elements in Garton the investigation was closed. So there was nothing any of us could do except sit back and watch him attempt to climb further up the promotion ladder. He was always ambitious and he'd had his eye on 'Executive Row' for a long time. For one thing, it would give him more clout with the drug gangs. Problem was, he knew that under the old chief constable he would never get promoted any higher. Not because he was being investigated, I'm quite certain he didn't know about that, but because Steve Morton had made it clear that Clayborn had gone as far as he was going. So when he heard the chief constable make that racist remark, Clayborn saw it as an opportunity to get rid of him. But he decided to do it without revealing who he was because he still had hopes of promotion under a new chief constable."

He paused to light a cigarette, cupping his hands against the wind to protect the match.

"And it all paid off when the new man was in place. Apparently, he liked Clayborn and when the vacancy for ACC came up he wanted him promoted. He knew that Clayborn had been investigated but, as he quite rightly pointed out, the man had been totally exonerated. But I was still running the investigation into the identity of the mole. That was why I didn't want Falcon messing things up. So I sowed the idea of the dream team to go after the Toybreaker. I thought that maybe Clayborn would object to Falcon serving as your deputy because it would give the Toybreaker investigation an edge. In the end, I needn't have bothered because Clayborn knew Falcon had been trying to find the mole himself and he was glad to get him out of the way. So for different reasons both Clayborn and I wanted the same thing. Falcon sidelined from the investigation into the identity of the mole. Anyway, I got enough evidence together to confront Clayborn. And when he realised how much I'd got on him he confessed that he had been the mole. But he refused to resign, taking the line that what he'd done was a public service. And he was prepared to tough it out, I'm certain of that."

He tossed the cigarette end onto the soil and ground it out under his heel before the dog could get to it.

"So it was time to play dirty. Clayborn's a disgrace to the service and I had no conscience about what I did next. I told him about the internal investigation. That shook him, but he recovered when he realised it had been dropped for lack of any real proof against him. Then I explained that there was, in fact, one particular piece of evidence that could be especially damaging to him. The section of video tape. On its own, of course, it was never going to be enough to prove anything, But I threatened to send it anonymously to the editor of the *Garton Evening News*. And that was enough because, for all his bluster, Clayborn didn't want that particular can of worms opened up. For the same reason, he didn't make an official complaint when you knocked him out."

He saw a stick on the path, bent down to pick it up, then threw it away onto the marshland. The dog hurled himself after it.

"So Clayborn's going?" That was one question Mallory felt he could ask.

"Yes, David, he's on his way. That's the upside. But the downside is that he goes on his terms. After full discussions with the chief constable, Clayborn is going to be allowed to resign with dignity on full pension. He will admit that he was the mole who exposed the last chief constable. He will also say that he did not reveal himself to be the source because he felt that if he did he would no longer be able to work on the force with the full confidence of his fellow officers. And that's why he's resigning now, because it has become known that he was the mole. And you have my permission to tell DCI Falcon before the official announcement is made. Tell him today. Might just be the boost he needs to enjoy New Year's Eve. Explain that he's in the clear with the rest of the force now. He deserves that."

"And Clayborn's resignation. No mention of his connection with the gangs?"

"Absolutely not. But that's politics. Sometimes, when you've gone as far as you can, you have to settle for a compromise. It's not perfect, but it's what someone once called the art of the possible. I hope it's a lesson you'll learn yourself."

"Me." Mallory grinned. "Oh, I don't think so. I'm sure it's only something you need when you reach the giddy heights of Executive Row."

"Quite so. And you know the set-up. One chief constable, one deputy chief constable and five assistant chief constables each with their own area of responsibility. A nice balance there, don't you think. But now, of course, with Clayborn gone there's a vacancy for an ACC Crime coming up. Could be good timing for you."

"What do you mean?" Mallory felt the shock run through him.

"Happy New Year, David."

The deputy chief constable smiled to himself as he walked away, leaving Mallory and the dog silhouetted against dark clouds of the late afternoon sky.

THE END

Thank you for reading this book. If you enjoyed it please leave feedback on Amazon, and if there is anything we missed or you have a question about then please get in touch. The author and publishing team appreciate your feedback and time reading this book.

Our email is office@joffebooks.com

www.joffebooks.com

We hate typos but sometimes they slip through.
Please send any errors you find to:
corrections@joffebooks.com

We'll get them fixed ASAP. We're very grateful to eagle-eyed readers who take the time to contact us.

18508255R00138

Printed in Great Britain
by Amazon